New England Mysteries

Book #1 - *A Cold Morning in MAINE,*

published in October, 2014.

ISBN 978-0-9962397-0-7

Book #2 - *A Quiet Evening in CONNECTICUT,*

published in April, 2015.

ISBN 978-0-9962397-1-4

Book #3 - *A Bad Night in NEW HAMPSHIRE,*

published in November, 2015.

ISBN 978-0-9962397-2-1

Bookstores, kindle and amazon – audio books

available from audible.com and iTunes.

www.nemysteries.com

a PIZZA NIGHT

in

the BAHAMAS

a PIZZA NIGHT in

the BAHAMAS

Terry Boone

ISBN 978-0-9962397-3-8

First Paperback Edition: November 2016

10 9 8 7 6 5 4 3 2 1

Published by
THREE RIVERS GROUP

Cover photo by the author.

a PIZZA NIGHT in

the BAHAMAS

This is a work of fiction. Names, places, events, timelines, distances and other information have been adapted or created entirely by the author. While some aspects of the story were inspired by real life experiences, far and away much of what you will read in this book is made-up. Any similarities to real people or to actual events and dates is *mostly* coincidental.

Published by **THREE RIVERS GROUP**

Contact: threeriversgroupvt@gmail.com

Walker's Cay

Little Abaco
Island

COOPERS TOWN

Manjack Cay

Green Turtle Cay
(New Plymouth)

Treasure Cay

Great
Guana
Cay

Man-o-War
Cay

Mores Island

The Marls

MARSH HARBOUR

Elbow Cay
(Hope Town)

Lubbers
Quarters
Cay

Gorda Cay

Little Harbour

Cherokee Sound

Sandy Point

Crossing Rocks

Hole in the Wall

For the good people and the

beautiful children of Abaco.

One
Friday, 11/11

It was a spectacular late afternoon on a magnificent beach. Soft breeze and a pleasant mix of fragrances from flowers on the dunes, the salt air and maybe the sunscreen I'd applied two hours earlier. Two small sail boats off on the horizon. An occasional gull swooping nearby.

Treasure Cay, Abaco. The Bahamas.

National Geographic once proclaimed this to be among the top ten beaches in the world: the subtle contrast of near white sand, pink flowers blooming year-round and the jaw dropping aquamarine expanse of water. It pegged the magnificent meter right up there at ten.

I'd been in a dream. Somewhere, more than a thousand miles away, but on a similarly bright day, out in fresh snow in the woods of Vermont.

Silvio, a sweet, old, soulful golden retriever that came to my house for the last three months of his life was in the dream. He was a younger, energetic dog in the dream and we were out in deep snow. On snowshoes, I couldn't keep up with him, so he would wait. As soon as I reached him and got my breath, he would give me the bright brown eyes and that classic golden retriever smile, then he would bolt away again. The dog really loved to run in the snow.

My face stuck to the towel on the beach chaise lounge. The sun was lower, but still bright. I squinted, cupped my right hand over my eyes and raised my head. The barely audible surf rolled in and out a few feet away. I sat up, adjusted the lounge to an upright position and put my sunglasses on.

Michael Hanlon is my name. I'm from Vermont, or, at least the last twenty-plus years. I recently turned fifty. Big deal, right? Not really. Mid-life? We'll see. But the timing coincided with a career change, from radio news reporter to private eye wannabe with a new vocation; Private Investigation/Background Security Services.

A divorce more than three years ago, a couple of recently successful forays into finding bad guys, along with one gunshot wound, and I have reached the point of moving on, as they say. Sometimes you wonder who *they* are? And who was the first one to offer the advice? In any event, the "*big*" birthday provided a good reason to accept an offer to rent a small cottage on this relatively undeveloped island only a one-hour flight east of Fort Lauderdale.

Further down the beach, two young kids – a boy and a girl - played at the edge of the water with their parents close by. The water was just this amazing Bahama blue unlike any color I have ever seen. Not azure, not teal, closer to turquoise. A blue that invited you to wade out as far as you dared.

An older couple approached slowly from the opposite direction, knee deep in the surf. Each of them carried a foam pool noodle, the kind you usually see people using in water fitness classes at an indoor pool.

The two kids splashed each other, the older girl taking the lead as provocateur. The boy, maybe four-years old, had water wings on his arms. I watched for a minute, then gathered my book, sandals and towel, shoved them in a canvas bag and prepared to walk back to the cottage.

There was a siren. It didn't sound like a siren in the US for police, fire, or ambulance. Nor a siren you heard in some French film: deh, dah...deh, dah. This was more of a loud, shrill, rapid ...whrrit, whrrit, whrrit. Each blip cut-off before it finished.

I scanned the others on the beach. Some people had heard it, some hadn't. The kids playing in the water heard it. They looked at their parents who also seemed to have heard it.

After only a few seconds, the siren abruptly stopped.

I knew the police station was close by in the center of the small island village, just across the street from where I was staying and a five-minute walk from the beach.

Dragging the chaise above the tide line I positioned it with a dozen others near a beach hut, all part of the resort community here. I rinsed sand off my feet next to the pool, put on the sandals and continued the short trek. No more sirens or sounds from down the street.

It was my third day on Abaco and I was beginning to adjust to the slow pace, the incredible weather and a 'no hurry' attitude exuded by just about everyone. Even the Bahamian children, none of whom were fooling with smart phones, displayed a mellow demeanor not often seen elsewhere.

Back at the two-bedroom cottage, temporarily mine thanks to the generosity of an old friend, I avoided turning on either radio or TV. There was a DVD player and some movies, as well as a collection of music CDs, but they could wait.

Ten minutes in the shower, a change into clean shorts and a tee shirt, and I felt more relaxed than I could recall in a long, long time.

Two
Atty

"Ah, mon! Dey got us," said Atty Gilbert. He leaned back against the wall, buried his face in his hands, shoulders hunched forward.

The siren stopped quickly. Atty knew that in just minutes that he would be in police custody.

"No, mon. Be still. Dey don't know we *here*," Joey Aberle whispered. He stood with his ear pressed to the door, gripping the handle.

Atty slumped to the floor. He sat motionless and looked up at Joey. "You *shoot* dem boys. Dey know *dat!*" Atty said, voice cracking and tears in his eyes.

In contrast, Joey's voice was deeper, slow and deliberate. He thought for a second maybe he would shoot Atty. He glared down at him. "Dey don't know who shoot dem boys. Dem boys *stupid*. Dey cheat us, mon."

Atty rolled his head from side to side, still covering his face with both hands.

Having entered a deluxe, canal front condo, Joey thought they were about to score some serious jewelry and maybe some cash. They'd watched the English couple for two hours. Joey was at a bar and heard the man say that he and his wife were on Abaco for an anniversary and planned to meet friends coming over by boat from West Palm Beach. The four planned to sail for a few days now that hurricane season was over.

Inside the condo for less than a minute, they heard the siren. Joey was cautious, Atty was scared. This was not what they imagined.

Only ten days earlier, in a late night encounter fifty minutes and fifty-some miles farther away, south of Marsh Harbour, Joey had exercised quick judgement when he shot two Haitian men who had failed to live up to an agreement for the purchase of a stolen boat. Atty had been a witness and a not very enthusiastic accomplice. The two Haitians and the 30-foot Grady White boat, were in police custody the next morning after the shooting occurred.

Located in the north of the Bahamas, less than two-hundred miles directly off the east coast of Florida, Abaco is comprised of two main islands, Great Abaco and Little Abaco. It's pronounced *abba*-co, like the pop vocal group. There are a dozen or so smaller islands and barrier cays, some with people and some without.

The two main islands cover an area less than a tenth the size of Vermont, which is ranked as the forty-fifth *smallest* state in the US. The combined population of all of the islands in the Abaco group is just under 18,000. In comparison, the seven-hundred islands in the chain of all of the Bahamas have a population of slightly more than 350,000 – still pretty small by most standards.

The Abaco islands were originally inhabited by the Lucayans well before Columbus et al cruised through. It didn't take long for a bunch of money-grubbing types to round up the natives and ship 'em out. Now, more than half a millennia later, like many places on earth, one thing has not changed: there are still good people and bad people. Judging others is risky business, but locals and tourists familiar with Abaco will quickly tell you that the good people *far* outnumber the bad.

The racial mix is believed to be about 50/50, black, or brown, and white. There are ex-pats from Europe and the US, as well as an influx of people from other Caribbean islands. On Great Abaco, the population density is concentrated at the southern end of the island in Marsh Harbor, with more than a third of the people residing there.

When it comes to criminal activity, much of that comes across the water from the more commercially developed islands. But there is some of the home grown variety, tool. Hence, one evolving local bad guy by the name of Joseph Aberle, aka "Joey".

Royal Bahamas Police Force Inspector Cynthia Knowles got out of the Jeep Wrangler and gazed across the parking lot. Constable Stephen Roos sat behind the wheel with the driver's door open.

"Been a long time," Inspector Knowles said. "Nothing changed." She smoothed her skirt, placed her hat on her head, slightly adjusting the fit. Roos got out of the right side of the Jeep from the driver's side, straightened his necktie and walked around to stand next to Knowles.

Late afternoon and the temperature was dropping from a high of 78. Only a slight breeze from the east.

No jewelry, no money, no arrests. The police did not come. Atty waited for Joey to motion him to the outside stairwell and away from the condo.

They slipped into Joey's pick-up truck and waited. There were no further sounds of the siren, no activity anywhere that they could see. Atty was convinced that the police were still out there, somewhere, maybe slipping up behind them at this minute.

Joey stared out the at the parking lot and the other cars. He didn't start the engine, but decided to wait for a few minutes to make the drive back to Marsh Harbour. Joey was anxious to get his hands on more cash. He would find a way to leave this island.

For the moment, stealing boats and robbing vacation rentals were not activities that he would continue to pursue.

Three
Back Then

An American couple coming out of the Golden Harvest grocery store looked over at the two policemen. Three young Bahamian boys huddled in the shade across the parking lot, remaining still, watching the two policemen. Spotting the boys earlier was why Roos had hit the siren briefly, which he had had to explain to the inspector that it was a little joke. She wasn't amused.

Knowles and Roos walked toward the closed office, Treasure Cay Branch, of the RBPF. It was located in the same small shopping plaza along with the grocery store, a bicycle and golf cart shop, a car rental business and a branch office of the Royal Bank of Canada. The RBPF office here had occasional visits from other members of the force, but this drop-by was unannounced.

Knowles pulled a key ring forward, inserted a key and unlocked the office. They both went inside. Constable Roos switched on a light. They stood for a moment with the door open.

"I started right here," she said, looking around the small office. One desk, a file cabinet, a raised counter like those used by ticket agents at an airport, and two chairs for visitors. There was a phone on the desk, an older tower computer hard drive on the floor and a small monitor with keyboard in the center of the desk.

Separate framed photos on the wall showed the current Prime Minister of the Bahamas, Perry Christie: the RBPF Commissioner, Ellison Greenslade: and two group photos of officers who presently served, or had served in the past, on Abaco. Knowles approached the photos.

"That's me. 1998," she said, tapping the glass of the lower group picture. Roos came over and looked at the photo. He thought the tall younger woman was attractive then, more so right now here in his presence.

"And this is Wesley Francis, my Sergeant," she said, pointing at a man in the center of the photo. "He became Superintendent." She paused, looking at the younger Roos, then added, "He died long before you were at the police college."

They both studied the photos for a minute. Knowles touched the glass on the group shot, then touched her shirt just above her heart.

"Let's go over to The Tipsy and see my cousin Romey," she said.

Roos went out first, Knowles followed. She left the light on and locked the door behind her. The three young boys were still watching the police Jeep. Roos pointed at them and gave a pretend salute.

The eldest in a family of eight children, Knowles

waved at the boys. They reminded her of three younger brothers at that age, maybe nine, ten and eleven years old. She walked toward the boys. The smallest of the three hugged the coconut tree. He looked at her with a shy expression and big eyes.

Bahamian children often could be spotted all around Treasure Cay and elsewhere on the island. This late in the day the boys were out of school. And the open, grassy area near the stores and parking lot was a regular stop for this trio.

"You boys are being good, yes?" Knowles asked. All three of them nodded in the affirmative.

Back when she was their age, a common sight was to see kids ranging in age from six to sixteen, wearing school uniforms, waiting for or just getting off a school bus. Now, fifty-plus years since some of the early and still relatively modest development of the island, the same scene played out each morning and afternoon.

Walking across the lot toward The Tipsy, she could only wonder what lay ahead for the children.

Four
Dolphinfish

On the menu in a restaurant it's mahi-mahi. Not to be confused with dolphins – that is the fully aquatic marine mammals – this sport fish can grow to thirty pounds and features brilliant colors, golden flanks with bright greens and blues on the back. The Spanish call them *dorado*.

On a really hot grill, when cooked properly, filets of dolphinfish can be just about the tastiest seafood going. At least away from some three-star restaurant in Paris. And while the term 'cooked properly' may be subjective, it had taken me a very short time on Abaco to learn that an essential part of getting the grill ready was to start with a bottle of Kalick, a popular Bahamian beer. One was ready for a second Kalick about the time the charcoal was ready.

I prefer my laptop over the smart phone for email, so I booted-up and logged-on. Nothing from Louie Ragsdale back in Vermont. In a phone call just before I left, we'd discussed the possibility of Louie and his wife coming down for a few days. Outside New England, he was a reluctant traveler.

I'd laid it on pretty thick about, 'How many times in your life is someone going to make a vacation house available to you for a month? In *November*.' I'd gone on to yak about how we could finally learn something about bone fishing, hire a local guide.

Ragsdale's response had been a tentative, 'Maybe. I'll talk to Becky.'

Right. And I was on a plane two days later, without hesitation, now trying to figure out how I could stretch my time away past Thanksgiving. Thinking about Louie's uncharacteristic ambivalence prompted me to fire off still another short email.

'Hey, just make a decision, guy. Pack a bag, drive to Burlington, get on a plane, eh? Really not that difficult. If Becky still has doubts, let's get on the phone.' I was pretty sure that any doubts were in Louie's head, not his wife's.

Using the chimney starter with three sheets of newspaper and lots of charcoal, I was thinking of all the advice and opinions I got from Louie nearly every time we talked. 'What you really should do,' or, 'I'm not sure that's the best way to,' etc. Yet I never heard him open up with others quite like that, which made me wonder how the interaction was in conversations with his wife.

One of his most recent wiseass opinions was about how I should prepare an ad to place in the next issue of *SSR Quarterly*. The publication *Search, Secure, Resolve* read like a magazine for a mixed audience of old soldiers of fortune, shopping mall security guards and would-be militia types. He gave me a back issue that he'd found during one of his undercover gigs. It was heavy on advertising and light on content. In a spoof email, Louie created and attached my ad all ready for insertion.

AVAILABLE: all-around Hotshot, likes baseball, women, soccer, movies, good food and wine. Middle age, middle brow, diplomatic and reasonably smart. Has gun, will travel throughout Northeast. Discreet. Oh yeah: likes to read, good voice and will record the outgoing message for your voicemail.

In a post script to the ad, he'd suggested that I could tack on: blue eyes, neatly trimmed beard, medium height, in shape, flaming Vermont liberal.

I went back to the kitchen to turn the fish in the marinade. The grill wouldn't be ready for another few minutes, so I replied to Louie that I was going to submit the ad just as he'd written it.

A gray, raw, wet afternoon in Vermont. Veterans Day, falling this year on a Friday, three days after the 58th quadrennial US Presidential election. And like many, Louis James Ragsdale was real happy to anticipate a little less political hype and maybe, however unlikely, *maybe* more civility and responsible adult behavior from those elected to federal offices.

Of course, there was also a chance that Elvis would be discovered alive and well, hiding in a monastery in the mountains of Kentucky.

Becky Ragsdale came in from the garage, pulled off her rain slicker and placed it on a hook near the door.

Louie was at the kitchen sink with his back to her.

"It's going to be like this for another week at least," she said. "I think we should go."

Louie wiped his hands on a towel, turned to face her and leaned against the counter. For maybe a full ten seconds, they stared at each other without a word. Finally, with just a trace of a smile, Louie raised both hands in the universal 'I give up' gesture.

"Sure. It's like Hanlon preaches, life is short. By all means, let's go to the Bahamas," he said.

"Do you think the kennel can take the dogs?" Becky asked. Louie nodded.

"Can't imagine they don't have room. Different story in two weeks." He went to the other end of the counter and picked up the phone. "Let's find out."

Using a fork and spatula juggling routine, I lifted the fish from the glass bowl and dropped it on the grill. The marinade – Newman's Own Italian Dressing, a little juice squeezed from a lemon, a shot of white wine, a dash of Tabasco Sauce and some salt and pepper – dripped and caused the charcoal to flame up and engulf the fish. I had a glass of water ready in case things got out of control.

While opening a second bottle of beer, the chime on my laptop signaled new email. It could wait a few minutes until I had the fish off the grill. In the fridge in a plastic bag was some left over green salad from last night. I dumped it into a bowl, put some of the dressing on it and sliced a loaf of freshly baked bread I'd purchased this morning.

The fish looked good, not overcooked. I lifted it to a plate and placed it on the round patio table next to the grill, unfolded my cloth napkin and sat to watch the sun dropping at the far end of the beach. Hold a gun on me and tell me that I have to live like this *every day* for the rest of my life. One should be so fortunate.

Five
Old Friends

The Tipsy Seagull is an open air restaurant and bar at the marina in Treasure Cay. Locals and returning tourists simply call it The Tipsy. Right on the canal and only a short walk from the beach, just the other side of the main street through the village, it is a popular venue for drinks, meals and also frequently music and dancing.

The summer before entering the Bahamas Police Academy in Nassau, eighteen-year-old Cynthia Knowles had worked at The Tipsy. As an all-around gofer for the resort manager, Avis Clarke, Cyndy became popular with the other staff members, due in large part to the fact that most of them had known her since she was a little girl. Cynthia's mother was a long-time food service employee at the resort. Nearly twenty years later, many of Cynthia's former co-workers – and one cousin – were still there.

When the two RBPF officers came up the boardwalk to The Tipsy, the bartender silently clapped her hands and greeted them with a bright smile. Cyndy offered her own little wave. Constable Roos took off his sunglasses and slipped them into the pocket of his shirt.

"Look at you," said the bartender, beaming and

gesturing with her arms extended as though she were presenting a gift. The RBPF Inspector shook her head at her cousin.

Romea Ellaine McIntosh, Romey for short, thirty-nine and two years older than Cynthia, was now the head bartender at The Tipsy and one of the most popular in all of Abaco. An observer might have guessed the two to be sisters, both with beautiful brown skin, high cheek bones, soft brown eyes and same smile that a generation earlier had made their mothers such attractive women.

Romey came from behind the bar and hugged Cyndy. She rocked her sideways and then released the embrace, leaning back to look at her.

"Why didn't you tell me you coming here, girl?" Romey said.

"I wanted it to be a surprise. Avis knows, but she promised not to tell. That's how I knew you would be working today," Cyndy replied.

"Will you see mama?" Romey's mother, the elder surviving sister of Cythnia's mother, was still in residence just a five miles from Treasure Cay.

"Yes. I'm going to be here for a week." Knowles turned to her colleague and introduced him.

"This is Constable Roos. My cousin and closest friend, Romea." They shook hands.

"Nice to meet you," Roos said.

"You as well," Romey responded, struck by how young the man looked. Could he really be twenty-one?

28

"Constable Roos is new to the force. We're going to be working together while I am here," Cyndy added.

"I finish at seven. Will you still be here?" Romey asked. Cyndy looked at her watch; 6:20. "Yes. I want to go say hello to Avis."

"Then can you come visit mama?"

"Of course. But I won't be able to stay long. We have to go to Cooper's Town."

"We wait. See what hawpen," Joey said. The two were in the front seat of an all-white, gold trim 1994 Toyota Tacoma, which also featured tinted glass all around. Easy to see out, difficult to see in. Radio playing low, windows cracked at the top. Just two guys hangin' out. No trouble, mon.

Atty fidgeted in the passenger seat. He played with the leather string of beads and shells around his neck, constantly rolling his head from side to side, a mannerism that Joey tolerated, but found very annoying.

"I *know* what hawpen. Dey put us in jail. Jus like Lil' Murph."

"Lil' Murph have a conch shell for da brain," Joey grumbled. This reply caused Atty to put his face in his hands again. He groaned and gave the impression that he would start crying in one second. Joey was tall, Atty was just big.

"Stop it, mon," Joey said as he slapped him on the

back of the head. Atty winced and pushed away from Joey, closer to the passenger door.

Turning the ignition, Joey switched on the headlights, slipped the truck into gear, crept out of the parking lot and eased onto the main street. He drove carefully beyond the traffic roundabout, past the security station entering Treasure Cay and out to the SC Bootle Highway that ran north-south the length of the main island.

Of all the guys Joey had ever spent any time with, he viewed Atty as being fragile. But fragile was not a word that Joey would use. Weak. Big baby, perhaps. Definitely not as tough as he should be. But they had known each other since the two of them skipped school more than ten years earlier to see The Baha Boyz, the touring squad of the national football team visiting Abaco.

When they were younger, Joey once felt as much pity as he now felt annoyance toward Atty. The pity is what prompted Joey to take Atty along after they'd been drinking together a couple times in recent months. But now, he couldn't imagine Atty being part of his future plans.

From the radio, *Money Machine* by Gucci Mane.

Six
Goombay Smash

Locking the door behind me, I headed for The Tipsy. Crossing the street, a white Jeep with the RBPF insignia on the driver's door passed going in the opposite direction, away from the village. Thinking back to the siren two hours earlier, I wondered what might've taken place. Guess we'll find out at the bar.

My friend, Bill Hancock, another old radio guy, owner of the cottage where I was staying, was a longtime visitor to Treasure Cay. He and his wife first came here back in the 1980s and returned a few times before purchasing one of the cottages ten years ago. When he suggested that I use their place for a vacation, I quickly accepted. He told me that one of the first things I should do when I got here was to visit The Tipsy and to try the trademark Bahamian cocktail, Goombay Smash.

Two nights ago when I arrived, I'd done just that. Normally, I'm a beer and wine guy not likely to go for mixed drinks, the occasional exception being a Margarita maybe during particularly hot weather. But now I wanted to quiz the bartender on the ingredients and proportions she used in mixing this fruity drink.

31

It was 6:30 when I took a seat at the bar. Light crowd, perhaps another fifteen people scattered around, including three others at the bar and the rest at tables.

"Something to drink?" the woman asked. The same bartender from two nights ago, same tropical, floral shirt worn by others I'd seen working at the resort, and she wore white pants and sandals. Friendly smile and laid back manner when she spoke.

"Think I'll try the Goombay Smash again." She nodded, smiled and turned to the long array of bottles lining a center counter above a sink.

I looked around at the crowd. The bar was oval shaped, possibly eighty feet in circumference. Directly across from me, ten or twelve feet away, were two women and a man. All three appeared to be late forties. Now that the sun had set, they all wore light weight sweaters. I'd brought along a sweater as well and draped it over the bar stool to my left.

Seated at different tables were a mix of people. Two older couples, laughing at something one of the men was saying. Four younger guys, maybe late twenties, drinking beer and looking at one of guy's smart phone. They struck me as most likely being from one of the boats in the marina. Then there were three more couples, two of them seated together at a table near the bar and the other pair sitting away from the center of the room, closer to the water.

The bartender returned and placed my drink on a

napkin in front of me. The clear plastic cup was filled to the brim and had a little straw in the center. I stirred the drink, removed the straw and took a sip. Cold, an appealing mix of fruit flavors and just a slight hint that there was alcohol in there, too. It was the kind of drink that could get you into trouble going down way too easy.

Louie Ragsdale could bring focus and order to anything he attempted. After waffling first with Hanlon, then with his wife, he had shifted completely to the 'get it done' mode and was knocking things off a mental checklist like it was his ballot in the election a few days earlier.

The kennel could take both of their dogs, an older male black lab and the younger rescue mutt, also a male. Louie would deliver the dogs in the morning. As soon as Becky said that she had found seats on an early Sunday flight to West Palm Beach with a connection to Abaco, Louie arranged for a room at one of the park and fly hotels. It was close to the Manchester, New Hampshire airport and alleviated the need to rise at 2:30 AM to drive four hours.

After a quick email to Hanlon saying that they were coming on Sunday, Louie brought a medium sized rolling duffle and two smaller carry-ons from the basement. He crossed his fingers that Becky would go light on things she needed for the trip. Surely they wouldn't need all three bags.

It would take him fifteen minutes to pack and he

would do it in the morning. Becky asked Louie to retrieve two plastic bins of warm weather clothing packed away for winter storage. She would take a bit longer to pack and would still be slipping stuff into the bag ten minutes before they left.

Thinking about fishing gear, Louie spent a few minutes online researching tackle that was best suited for bone fishing. Depending on which blog you believed, the choices ranged from the minimalist view - rod, reel and a small selection of salt water flies with maybe a back-up rod – to the gear-head safari approach, as in, how much can you carry?

He actually made a list of things that he would need to do after dropping the dogs off, including a reminder of two phone calls regarding work scheduling for later in the month. Unlike the erratic routine when he was on assignment as an undercover drug cop, Louie tried to practice 'early to bed, early to rise' at home. By 7:30, he was ready for a shower and a few minutes of watching the news on TV before hitting the rack.

Rebecca Ragsdale, everyone but her mother called her Becky, had a slightly different way of dealing with tasks than the method practiced by her husband.

With anything beyond daily routine, especially if it was something a bit out of the ordinary flow of events, Becky was deliberate and thoughtful. Think, look, think some more, act carefully. Never in haste. And check again. Did I leave the iron plugged in?

As that mindset became fully engaged, Becky sat down with a cup of tea and began making notes of all that she needed for the trip. Rather than just cram things into a duffle, she would lay everything out on the bed, neatly folded, before selecting what to pack and what to leave behind.

I watched the bartender. More people were arriving. All of her movements seemed natural and effortless, certainly not hurried. It reminded me of watching really good athletes who give the impression that this was just a game to be *enjoyed*, that they were confident of their ability to control the game and that *you*, as a spectator, should just lighten-up and enjoy it, as well. And she was lovely.

"Can you tell me about the Goombay, or is it some house secret?" I asked when she came to my side of the bar.

Great smile, a tilt of the head. Was that a wink?

"It has been around a for a very long time," she replied. Her voice carried genuine warmth underscored with a distinct Bahamian accent.

"What's the rum, dark or light?"

She waggled a finger at me like I'd said something naughty.

"There are many variations. We use a mix of coconut and dark rum, a little apricot brandy and pineapple juice." She leaned her elbows on the bar, closed her hands into loose fists and placed them under her chin. Leaning her head slightly forward, her face was approximately sixteen inches from mine. She raised her eyebrows and added, "At home, I also use slices of banana that I soak in the rum for a few minutes before I mix in pineapple juice."

She held my gaze for a couple of seconds, tapped the side of my plastic cup, then pushed off the bar and left to endure comments from other customers.

Maybe twenty per cent of my drink remained, about one inch at the bottom. It was definitely having an effect. I wasn't sure about the Goombay part, but felt that it would not take much more for the smash to kick in.

Seven
North Abaco

At the north end of Great Abaco is the main office of the Royal Bahamas Police Force for the island and all of the smaller cays close by, known as the "family islands".

Inspector Cynthia Knowles grew up in the village of Cooper's Town. With a population under eight hundred, a former Prime Minister of the Bahamas had a home there as well. Recently, it had gained attention as the site of a controversial new deep water port being developed by a state-owned firm from China at a cost of $40 million. Some locals questioned the need and the wisdom for such an enterprise.

For the next week, the village would be hosting ten rising stars in the RBPF in a series of workshops, lectures and psychological testing exercises, designed for future leaders of the government's *Working Together for a Safe Bahamas* initiative. Should word get out to the media about the timing and location of these sessions, reporters and pundits would have a field day speculating on the enduring friendship and loyalties between the RPBF Commissioner and the *former* PM.

Knowles was one of those rising stars and had clearly

earned the trust of her superiors, so much so that the Commissioner and other senior staff back in Nassau were easily persuaded to use the remote location for this particular training. Knowles had arranged to arrive two days early.

As a bright but somewhat shy school girl, as well as an outstanding basketball player, 'Cyndy' developed into a composed, confident and determined young woman. Following her education through high school, she went off to the Police College and graduated in the top of her class. Serving in remote postings for six month periods, rising through the ranks from constable to corporal, and then a sergeant, she had been promoted to Inspector at the end of 2015.

On the short drive from Treasure Cay, Inspector Knowles quizzed the younger Constable Roos about what he remembered from his classes on the history of the police force.

Feeling a trace of perspiration on the back of his neck, gripping the steering wheel and locking his eyes on the road in front of him, Roos hated these questions. He was capable, fit and would likely become a good officer. History, however, was not his strongest suit. Remembering names and other details of the formation of the first law enforcement in this island nation was a bit of a challenge.

"Slaves," he finally offered.

"Good," replied Knowles. "That is right. Almost two-hundred years ago when the first Police Force was organized under the Inspector General on New Providence, they were *all* former slaves. That group of men had one of my ancestors from my mother's side."

As Knowles chatted on about the history and growth of the RBPF, Roos slowed as he entered the village. The designated buildings were less than a half-mile ahead on the right.

The plan was for Knowles to check in, meet briefly with an Assistant Superintendent and discuss preliminaries for the training session scheduled to begin early Monday morning.

Still at The Tipsy, I worked-out what my next line would be for the bartender. Ask her about the blue holes. Pacing myself, watching the crowd and the dancing, and knowing that I would be walking home and not driving, I waited a full ten minutes before I motioned to her that I was ready for a second Goombay.

The first night when I had arrived at the cottage, I stayed up late reading about the island. There was a quarterly magazine called *Abaco Life*, of which there were about three years of back issues in the living room; a copy of *Bahamas Living*, really aimed at tourists and would be home buyers; some history books on Abaco and other islands; and an August, 2010 issue of *National Geographic* with a feature story and some great underwater photos of the caves and canyons of Bahamas Blue Holes.

"Are any of the blue holes close by?" I asked as she placed the drink in front of me.

Her face brightened and eyebrows arched. "Yes. Very close," she said.

"Really?"

"Did you fly into Treasure Cay?"

"I did."

"There is one near the airport." She was doing the elbows on the bar, hands under the chin routine again. Another bartender, also a woman, had arrived earlier and drink orders were under control. "Can you wade out, or do you need a boat?" I asked.

"No. It is on the island. You can drive. Or take a bicycle. Very easy."

"Really?"

"You like that word. *Real-ly*," she exaggerated, then laughed.

For a second, I felt self-conscious. She patted my arm and laughed again.

"I am only teasing you. Everyone has an expression they use often." The smile was playful, not like she was laughing *at* me. Having fun, not making fun. Or at least I chose to interpret it that way.

"Do you know what I say all the time?" she asked.

"Can't imagine." I took a sip of the drink.

She waited a beat, glanced around to be sure that no

one was waiting to place an order, then slowly wiped the bar in front of me with a towel.

"I don't believe it," she said.

"Don't believe what?"

"*That's* what I say. 'I don't believe it.' My mama says it will be on my tombstone. 'She didn't believe it'." She laughed and shook her head.

"What's your name, by the way?" Smooth, Hanlon.

"Romey."

I held out my hand. "I'm Michael. Nice to meet you." We shook.

"It is nice to meet you, Michael. Please, do not be offended by my teasing."

"Not at all. Really."

Eight
Central Abaco

A new airport, ferries to other islands, retail hub.
Those words could be a text message to someone deciding
where to land on Abaco. In fact, most visitors who fly to
the island come into Marsh Harbour. It is also where some
of the natives depart for other islands or to the US.

Near the center of the town, Joey Abere slept until
noon. When he awoke, Atty was nowhere to be seen,
already out somewhere, maybe gone back to his sister's.
Rising from the bed slowly, Joey went to the bathroom, got
dressed and prepared to head out himself. He would go
find Benji and not worry about Atty.

Benji was a taxi driver in Marsh Harbour. This man not
only knew the likes of Joey Aberle, but possibly knew
everyone who'd been on the island for more than a year.

Benji, whose real name was Benwald, was of mixed
parentage, short and stocky, in his late 50s, gregarious
and resourceful. He was also a kind person. Helping
someone like Joey was no different from helping a

passenger carry groceries from the store, or helping older people move furniture and heavy objects in their homes.

On more than one occasion, Joey had heard Benji speak of his son who now lived and worked on Grand Bahama. While Joey knew others with some connection to the resort island, it was almost certain that the RBPF knew them, too. And not because they were supporters of police charitable events. Bigger crowds on Grand Bahama near Christmas. That was just over a month away. Joey would find a way to get there.

Also near the center of town – away from the water, the ferry dock and boat slips, away from the tourist oriented businesses and restaurants – are two run down communities located side-by-side. Home to hundreds of illegal migrants, one community is known as Pigeon Pea and the other is just called The Mud. Located right off Queen Elizabeth Drive and only a stone's throw from a branch of the Royal Bank of Canada, the area will not be featured in any vacation brochures.

Pigeon Pea is the older community. The Mud got its name from the fact that it is a low-lying area and the first place to flood during heavy rains. This less desirable section, covering just a few acres, is a five-minute walk from Joey's tiny second floor apartment in Marsh Harbour.

Both shanty town communities have grown in size and population in recent years, predominantly inhabited by Haitian immigrants. Small, overcrowded dwellings patched together with scrap wood or materials not normally used for building, with flimsy scrap metal roofs. Where electricity exists, wires are strung, sometimes through trees, from one structure to the next. Most of the dwellings are duplex or triplex and most of the people living in them are believed to be in the country illegally.

Unlike many of his fellow natives of Marsh Harbour, Joey occasionally visited The Mud. Some of the men he encountered in his social life were Haitians who live there. More than once, he had gone to dance parties held at non-licensed establishments in the community.

The best places to go look for Benji were either the pubic docks where ferries came in and out, or near the market on the edge of town. Joey headed for the docks.

As many as twenty ferries a day leave Marsh Harbour for nearby islands. In addition, there are charter trips departing and arriving. Locals and tourists, coming and going, many needing a taxi when they step onto the dock.

The taxis, normally some type of van that might accommodate five passengers and their luggage, are in great supply in both population centers on Abaco. Because of the newer airport terminal and the ferries, most taxis use Marsh Harbor as their hub. From here, the longest trip might be just under one-hundred kilometers, or sixty miles, out to the northwestern tip at Cooper's Town or Crown Haven. The majority of the trips run between here and Treasure Cay, or a short drive to the south end of the island.

Similar to cabbies all over the world, the men and women taxi drivers on Abaco spend a lot of time sitting in their vehicles waiting for the next fare. They don't normally get out and socialize with other drivers. They might check things on their van, or wipe a fender or clean the interior. They generally spend a lot of down time with their radio and other forms of audio entertainment.

Benji was listening intently to an afternoon broadcast on *Joy 101.9 FM*, a gospel station from Nassau. His return party would be coming in twenty minutes on the next ferry back from Hope Town. Joey spotted Benji's van parked in the shade next to three other taxis. He walked in that direction.

Atty Gilbert listened to his sister, keeping his head down avoiding eye contact. At forty, Mirella was the eldest of nine siblings. Atty, the youngest, was now twenty-four. All the way back to the time he was an infant, Mirella was as much a parent to him as their real mother. Some things never change.

"My Junior is more responsible dan you! He is jus twenty-one and is no goody boy. But he will *not* go to jail. His daddy see to him first," Mirella said. "Not like you, TD quick to learn not to do same dumb things over and over."

Atty didn't look up. He knew his sister's lectures, knew the inflection and her facial expressions, knew when not to reply. This was one of those times. It was a mistake to have told her even just a little about his friendship with

45

Joey. Now she was letting him have it.

Arms folded, eyes wide and a scowl that would intimidate the toughest bone fish guide on the island, which her husband reputedly was, Mirella wanted to cry. More than once it had occurred to her that there was hardly a week when she *didn't* want to cry. It was always something with Atty. If he lived to be eighty, he would still be thirteen.

But Mirella would hold on. She would finish her scolding, fix her little brother some lunch, hug him and pray that, perhaps this time, he would take just a little of her advice. This time, perhaps, his fear would be sufficient to get him on a better path.

"You can stay here 'til Terrence comes back. If you do not annoy him, maybe you can stay tonight. If he thinks that you are drinking, if he thinks that you are still friends with that Joey, he will not let you stay here," she said. "I am going to work in one hour and will not be home until late."

Atty raised his head enough to look at her. His eyes were welling up, but he was able to hold back the tears and pull up a smile. As often happened, it melted her heart.

Nine
MHT Airport

"He knows what time our flight arrives?" Becky Ragsdale said. Louie nodded in the affirmative. Too early in the morning to chat, at least for Louie if not for his wife.

Up at 4:30 was not the problem. Getting the luggage down to the hotel lobby and onto the airport shuttle for a 6:55 flight was no big deal either, although he was not looking forward to the line at the gate and the TSA security routine still to come.

It was being cheerful. He just couldn't do it, especially early in the day. Never Louie's strongest response, it was an attitude adjustment impossibility this early in the day. Too many years in the army, then a municipal cop, now an undercover drug enforcement agent. Early mornings were good for lots of things and often it was his favorite time of the day. Just don't ask him to be jolly.

Now enroute to the terminal, Becky patted his leg.

"I'm really excited," she said. Again the nod from Louie.

"Did you check the forecast? Still calling for sunny all week?" Louie looked at her.

Seated across the aisle and fooling with his phone was one other man on the courtesy shuttle with them. The man pretended not to listen. Maybe he was not Mister Happy in the morning either.

"Near 80 every day. 68 at night," Louie answered.

"I packed the sunscreen. 50 spf. How about insects?" Becky said. Louie shrugged and shook his head.

"I don't think so."

Louie Ragsdale and his wife were on a flight due in at 2:30 at the Treasure Cay airport. Pretty small, but it had the 'international' designation. I would get a taxi to be there to meet them, which gave me plenty of time to shop for food, work online, go to the beach, do whatever I wanted for the next six hours.

First stop: Café La Florence for coffee and a cinnamon bun about the size of a bible. Bill had warned me that the buns were a little too sweet for his taste. I was confident that I could handle it as I had two days earlier. This morning I would muster the courage to give it another go.

Other vacationers were in and out of the café getting coffee and something sweet. Two men, locals I guessed, sat inside talking over coffee. I placed my bun and a napkin at an outside table, went back in to get the coffee and the most recent copy of *the abaconian*, a free, twice-monthly newspaper.

On the front page, above the fold, was a photo of the

Right Honourable Perry Christie, the current Prime Minister, addressing a financial services conference held on the island a week ago. I read about his reaction to the recent news of the World Bank dropping the Bahamas' ranking on the list of countries rated for 'Ease of Doing Business.'

According to the report, the Bahamas was now at 106. Out of how many countries was not reported. Other stories included: Collision Injures Four; Long Time Civil Servant Retires; Landscaping at the Mini-Hospital; and What Can You Find at the Treasure Cay Market? It took me only a few minutes to go through all thirty-two pages in two sections, ample time to eat the bun and finish my coffee.

The blue sky was clear and the day looked promising. I was weighing the appeal of sitting for a while and having more coffee, watching people, versus a short walk to the beach and the same blue sky, plus the amazing view across the open water.

I took a last swallow of coffee and thought about the previous night's conversation with Romey the bartender. I recalled that she told me about the blue hole located not far from the airport. Carrying my empty mug and paper plate back inside, I asked Florence how far it was out to the blue hole.

"It is not far. Before you come to the airport," she said. "There is a road that goes into the woods."

"Is there a sign?" I asked.

"No sign," one of the men at the table behind me said. I turned to face him.

"Perhaps one mile, a little more into the woods. If you get to a farm, too far. Before that," he added.

"Suppose I can get one of the taxi drivers to take me?"

"Yes. I can take you. I have a taxi," he replied.

Romey McIntosh fretted over the talk she'd had last night with her friend Mirella. Hearing Mirella worry about her younger brother, Atty, brought back painful memories of a former boyfriend of Romey's who left the island years ago.

She never heard from him after he left. It was before cell phones became so cheap that everyone had one. And she missed him for a long time. He was sweet, funny, kind and before falling into a bad drug habit, he made Romey believe that she might marry him one day.

Almost a year after the boyfriend left Abaco, she learned that he'd been killed outside a bar in Florida. It was the summer when Cyndy worked at the resort. After telling her cousin about the news, she had cried most of that night. She had had sporadic bouts of emotional distress for weeks. Then, and now, no matter what or when the memories came to her, she never spoke of him to anyone.

Pulling on a pair of open toe sandals, Romey finished

her coffee and got ready for the short drive into Treasure Cay center. It was a day off, but she frequently spent an hour or so free time at the resort checking bar supplies needed for the following week and looking over the work schedule.

Ten
Loyalists

The taxi driver at Café La Florence gave me his business card. Reggie Sayle. The card had a photo, his assigned license number ID and both a home and mobile phone number. We talked about a trip out to the blue hole later in the week, but for now he agreed that he would pick me up at two o'clock for this afternoon's run to the airport.

I walked over to the market to buy some groceries to have when the Ragsdales arrived. Ten minutes and less than forty dollars later I was out the door. Walking across the lot on my way back to the cottage, an older dark green Honda Accord coupe pulled into a parking space just ahead of me. Out from behind the wheel stepped Romey. I noticed her white slacks and the sandals first. She waved.

"Good morning," I said, walking over to where she'd parked. I got the smile.

"Cooking for yourself?" she said, pointing at my grocery bag.

"Yes. And I have friends arriving this afternoon."

"That's nice. Is it their first visit to Treasure Cay?"

"Yep. And it was a *hard sell* to get them to come."

She cocked her head and gave me a puzzled expression. "They do not like beautiful places?"

"Oh, I don't think that's the issue. I'm sure they'll like it when they get here. They, at least the husband, who is my friend, don't really travel a lot outside of New England."

"Ah." She held the car door open while we talked. "Tell me, why is it called New England? You are from Vermont, yes?"

"Goes back to the Pilgrims landing there four-hundred years ago. Then a bit later on, others, mostly from England, began settling the colonies which now are the six states of the northeastern corner of the US." Romey folded her arms and gave the appearance of being interested, so I babbled on. "They didn't like a lot of what the Church of England was doing back in the day." I raised my arms to the sky. "Sailed across the Atlantic and, a few generations later, mostly in the New England colonies, revolted against the British government."

"That was your American Revolution?" she said.

"Correct. The Declaration of Independence, July 4th, fireworks, parades, hot dogs and all that."

"And those in your colonies who did *not* want to leave the British government. Do you know where they went?" Her expression changed to what many reporters and politicians think of as 'gotcha'. I pointed in the direction of the beach.

"Right over there. Mostly from the South. But some from New York." I laughed and said, "Good 'ol loyalists." Brand new history lesson for me, thanks to some of what I'd read only three nights ago.

"Yes. Many of your 'loyalists' came to Abaco. Hope Town, then some of the other islands."

"You could be related to some of them," I said.

"I do not *think* so," she replied with a chuckle, reaching back into the car and retrieving a straw handbag.

Other members of the RBPF training session began arriving late Sunday morning. On hand to greet them was Inspector Cynthia Knowles, self-appointed local emissary. Not really the leader for the week ahead but acting more as the Commissioner's liaison.

Knowles would greet most of them when they showed up in Cooper's Town and then all of the participants would have dinner. Having spent the previous day visiting with her aunt and other relatives close by, she was now back into a professional mode. It was a demeanor that others might expect in an officer much older and with more years on the force. Beyond her obvious skills and intelligence, senior officers back in Nassau saw it as a clearly defined, always sharp, no-nonsense attitude and that she always conveyed the 'move it forward' approach to any task or challenge.

Contrary to her calm appearance at the moment, psychologically, Cynthia Knowles was pumped-up and ready to go.

She had reviewed the entire schedule for the training and knew that the first three days would be long and intense, running from 7:30 AM to 6 PM. Some outside physical training on Thursday would be a shorter session, to be followed by a social evening when everyone could kick back a couple of notches. There would be a shorter review and critique on Friday morning.

With this schedule in mind, and after earlier consultation with Romey, Knowles had a treat planned for her fellow officers on Thursday evening: a drive down to Treasure Cay for Pizza Night.

While some in the training group had either previously served on or had visited the island, it was pretty certain that they all had heard of Pizza Night. Billed as 'Abaco's Largest Social Event,' the gathering every Thursday night of the year was held next to the marina in Treasure Cay at The Tipsy Seagull.

Anticipating her first visit to the event in more than ten years, Inspector Knowles had a promise from Romey that a table would be reserved for the RPBF contingent. They'd both laughed at the likely reaction of other patrons if a group of police officers arrived en masse for a few pizzas. Knowles assured her cousin that the group would be wearing plain clothes and not in uniform.

Eleven
FLL to TCB

Watching other passengers at the gates in the boarding area of the Fort Lauderdale-Hollywood International Airport reminded Louie of *why* he hated flying. Aside from the claustrophobia of being tightly packed into seats too close together inside a machine that he had no control over, he really didn't enjoy being around a crowd numbering more than a dozen or so people.

Staring at the boarding pass that assigned him to seat 14E on Silver Airways flight 94 connection to Treasure Cay, Bahamas, Louie wondered if 14E was an aisle or window seat. Becky could have the window, thank you. He also wondered what kind of plane would carry the passengers of flight 94, how many seats, how many emergency exits, would he have to complete a customs form before landing on Abaco?

The boarding pass read departure 1:30 and arrival 2:33 PM. Barely more than an hour to fly 180 miles out into the ocean. Lower down on the pass it indicated the aircraft was a Saab 340. A Swedish plane? So they don't make cars anymore but *do* make airplanes? Louie's knowledge of aircraft manufacturers started and stopped with Boeing. He suspected that Hanlon knew about the different planes and would quiz him about this later.

"Where did you get these tickets?" he said to Becky.

"Kayak," she said. Louie raised his eyebrows.

"It's one of a bunch of online services. They work with the airlines trying to sell limited numbers of unsold seats. They discount the rates. We saved $200 roundtrip from Fort Lauderdale. Another option was from West Palm Beach, but the flights only go to Marsh Harbour."

Louie continued his study of the boarding pass. Over the years Becky had seen him do the same thing with concert and sporting events tickets, looking at them as though he might discover some hidden meaning or significant information unknown to anyone else.

"And we come back on Friday?" he asked.

Becky held her patience. She knew that *he* knew the day and time of the anticipated arrival back in New Hampshire and the drive back to their home in northeastern Vermont.

"You said that you couldn't stay any longer." It was her turn for the raised eyebrows. "When we talked about coming, you *said* that you had things to do next weekend before going back to work."

He did have things to do, but they would take all of about one hour. He just didn't want to be away from home longer than a week.

Louie watched the other passengers some more. He was especially annoyed by a man two rows over who was being way too loud. Christ, if he's in this boarding area, he's on our flight.

"I'd like to try snorkeling," Becky said. Louie turned back to her.

"You do remember I'm not a good swimmer."

"I'm sure they have people all the time who don't swim."

"So, they drown them?"

She shook her head and turned back to an older copy of *Vanity Fair* with a feature on Queen Elizabeth's ninetieth birthday.

80°F and sunny. The baggage handlers all wore shorts and short sleeve shirts. More than fifty pieces of luggage being hand-shifted from two carts into the cargo hold of a twin-engine turbo prop headed for Treasure Cay, Abaco.

These guys were good and often times had to bring bags from connecting flights only a few minutes apart. Loading the smaller planes could be a real challenge because of limited space and because many passengers frequently didn't consider the size of their bags. Even with weight restrictions and added fees, people still brought along way more than they needed. 'TMFS' was a code among veteran baggage handlers; too much fucking stuff.

You often heard it from the last handler in line trying to pack all the bags into a smaller plane.

Push back from the gate at 1:26 PM. A young woman in shorts and the airline issued logo shirt, worn under a bright yellow synthetic vest, also wearing ear protectors and waving bright orange wands as she directed the pilot. A manifest of thirty-four passengers, two pilots and additional crew of two attendants, ready to depart.

Another five minutes talking with Romey McIntosh in the parking lot and I was able to: a) learn that she did not have a significant other; b) that she also had Wednesdays off; and c) I got her phone number.

I walked to the cottage, put away groceries and still had time for the beach before going to the airport. Pulling the chaise close to the soft, even, outgoing tide, I remembered that I never found out what the siren was all about two days earlier. Couldn't have been much or I likely would have heard by now. Then, maybe not. No local radio in TC and the island newspaper was published every two weeks. If it ain't important, you don't need to know.

Hanlon goes PI in the Bahamas. What, who, when, where, why? And how? *Wait*, that's what Ragsdale calls 'Radio Rick' stuff. Maybe when he gets here I'll make up some phony story about a big drug bust at the marina. Helicopters, police dogs sniffing around boats, nude sun bathers. Sorry you missed it.

Twelve
Joey

"Maybe I can find work," Joey had said. He was lying. And there was a pretty good chance that Benji had *known* that he was lying, but Joey hadn't cared. He was beginning to feel desperate.

That was yesterday when Joey had spoken with Benji at the docks in Marsh Harbour, asking Benji to put him in touch with his son on Grand Bahama. While some kind of employment might be considered, Joey simply needed to get off Abaco. Soon.

Benji had taken Joey's cell number and said that he would give it to his son, who worked long hours and different shifts at a resort. No telling when he could call.

One of Joey's acquaintances from The Mud told him that the two Haitians who'd been shot over the stolen boat deal had not been welcomed, at least not by the people he knew. The men were rumored to have been runners connected to a large and dangerous drug smuggling network. The two had also been reported to be striking out on their own with Abaco as the first break-away initiative.

Word that one of the men had since died after being arrested had not made it to the public. Or to Joey.

While he was aware of the drug trafficking angle, there was no way to know how much stock to put in this man's opinion. On the other hand, Joey was pretty certain this man couldn't know that Joey had been the shooter. But Atty knew. And that was a problem.

Stay here, with the increasing risk that the RBPF would make the connection and arrest him for both stealing the boat and shooting two men, or get away as soon as possible to another island, maybe the US. The choice was not difficult.

Sitting on a bench watching tourists reminded Joey of another possibility. He recalled a story from two years ago when a man living in Marsh Harbour allegedly took hire on a freight ship and made it into the US without a passport. Joey recalled what the man looked like and that he was not originally from Abaco. He thought about the story and, true or not, he couldn't recall seeing the man in more than a year now. Maybe the story was true.

He stood to begin the walk back to his apartment. While he could hope to hear from Benji's son, what he needed more than anything was a plan that offered more immediate promise.

Atty had always been frightened of his brother-in-law. Terrence D. Williams, Senior was a big man – over six feet and more than two-hundred pounds – and he had a big voice. When Atty was little, he would often hide when this boyfriend came to see Mirella.

More than twenty years hadn't changed much. Terrence was still big and Atty was still afraid of him. But now he was in the man's house. One misstep and it would be like his sister told him, he would not let him stay. Now here they were together. Atty believed that Terrence might even call the police.

"You still not wit dat bum Joey?" Terrence declared more than asking. Atty shook his head.

"He is no good. You ask Mirella about Joey Aberle." Terrence slowly rubbed his hands as though he was washing them with disinfectant.

"I tell Mirella dat you can stay. You are like TD, another son to her."

Still no reply. Not a small guy himself, Atty hunkered like a frightened little potcake.

"I will be sleeping early tonight. Go to Eluthera wit two Englishmen tomorrow, chase da bone fish. If you go out, don't be stayin late. Mirella she will come find you when she get home." Terrence gave him the look with this last piece of advice.

Atty shifted his gaze back to the television and tried not to think about Joey. But Joey had promised him some money after the boat deal. Before the Haitians had been shot in the argument over what they would pay, Atty knew that Joey had accepted some cash from them. How much, Atty didn't know. But it was a wad of bills that Joey had counted before the yelling and swearing started and the confrontation turned violent. Then the shots.

Mirella Williams was *not* afraid of her husband, despite his size and the frequent menacing stares and the silence when something didn't please him. The early years of the marriage had been a bit stormy, but Mirella long ago had reeled Terrence in.

Both were diligent and hard workers at their jobs, strong on love of family unity, and they were devoted to one another. While both could be stubborn and feisty, especially in dealing with any lapse in self-discipline or frequent distraction exhibited by their only son, and the occasional disagreements over relations with each other's family members, Mirella and Terrence shared a physical desire and passion that went back to their youth. When it came to intimacy, they were still twenty-year-olds.

It had been many years ago, shortly after TD, Junior had started school, when Terrence had had a brief stretch of no guiding work with sportsmen and he'd spent most of several weeks at home. When he finally got back to steady bookings and work with another fishing guide from a near-by island, every time he left the house he and Mirella would spend a few minutes kissing and groping. Before he was out of sight, she would pretend to be reeling a fish in and blow him a kiss as he went off to the truck.

Working now as a housekeeping supervisor at the resort in Treasure Cay, she could still - and often did -

clean rooms, change beds, stock fresh towels and toiletries and show the younger women how to do things correctly.

Mostly because of their proximity in age and having spent many years working at the resort, Mirella and Romey McIntosh had become close friends. And they often confided in one another. So Mirella was not surprised when Romey, on a day off from work, came looking for her simply to ask how things were going.

"Mirella, let's go sit for a bit," Romey said.

Holding up a finger to indicate wait, Mirella went down the corridor and into a vacant guest room to speak to a young woman cleaning. When she returned, she patted Romey's cheek and they went for a chat.

Thirteen
Sunscreen

The Treasure Cay Airport terminal is small, there's one long runway and the buildings are dated. But the staff is professional, welcoming without being phony, and very efficient.

After a wave to let them know that I was there, it took only five minutes for Louie and Becky Ragsdale to clear customs and get their luggage. Reggie Sayle was quick to load the bags in the rear of his taxi and we headed back to TC. Before we got onto the highway, Becky had a tube of sunblock out and was applying some to her face and arms.

Shifting his eyes back and forth and controlling the smirk, Louie wiggled his thumb toward his wife without her seeing the movement. They were in the backseat and I was turned facing them from the left front passenger seat.

"Good idea," I said to Becky. "I was at the beach before you got here and the sun is still pretty strong. Hard to believe that it's November."

"Isn't it going to be dark in what, two hours?" Louie

said, looking at his watch. Becky gave him a wife-type elbow and continued applying the cream.

"You remember that Kurt Vonnegut story that went around on the internet a few years ago about a commencement speech?" I said.

Louie gave just the slightest shake of his head. Becky said, "No. But I love Kurt Vonnegut."

"The story went around that he gave this great commencement speech at MIT, with thoughts on what's really important in life, things new graduates should do and things they might want to avoid," I said. "He started with, 'If I could offer you only *one* tip for the future, sunscreen would be it.' He offered nuggets of wisdom and humor, but concluded with, 'Trust me on the sunscreen.'

"It was a real hit," I continued. "People were talking about it, it got a lot of write-ups in newspapers around the country. The only problem, Vonnegut never gave the speech. A columnist for *The Chicago Tribune* composed it as a speech that she would *like* to give."

No reaction from Louie. Becky laughed, closed the cap on the sunblock and put it in her bag.

"And," I added, "the post script was that, allegedly, when Vonnegut found out about it, he said that he really liked it and wished that he had written it."

"So, allegedly, can we look this up?" Louie said.

"Be my guest. Probably find it with music links to the greatest hits of the 90s."

At 5:20 we watched the sunset. Louie and I joined Becky at the beach. She took his hand and we walked along the surf for fifteen minutes before turning back to the cottage. It was warm, still in the 70s. It would cool down pretty quickly now that sun was gone.

"Hanlon's going to fix dinner on the grill," Ragsdale said.

"Unless you want to go out," I chimed in.

Becky looked at me. "No, great. What are we having?" she said.

"I got some frozen filets from this fishing guide that my friend Bill put me in touch with. I had some two nights ago and it was outstanding. I put it in some marinade earlier today."

Before coming to find Becky, Louie and I stayed back talking about fishing possibilities, the weather and how amazing I found this place to be. Other than a brief exchange about guides, boats, bone fish flats and the gear we had between us, I'd done most of the talking. This was a pretty normal pattern. And while I always reverted to calling him Louie, he usually called me 'Hanlon'. Or, Radio Rick. Or some mild but unflattering profanity.

Once we got back to the cottage I began preparing dinner. Becky seemed mildly perturbed that her husband had only placed their bags on the bed and had not yet unpacked his, so Louie got it in gear and began putting things in drawers. There were matching bureaus in each bedroom and like most of the furniture, the bureaus were made of wicker painted white.

Waiting for the charcoal to get hot, Louie and I had a beer. Becky poured a glass of white wine. We sat in the living room and I gave them an abbreviated rundown on what I'd learned so far about things to do, places to go.

"I want to go snorkeling," Becky said. "Can we do that here, or do we have to travel to another part of the island?"

"I'm not sure. But we can find out in the morning. There's a marina. Somebody will know." I felt a little dumb that I hadn't already checked on this after having leaned on them to make the trip. If Louie had enthusiasm for the snorkeling idea he was keeping it under control.

"If we actually want to go out with a guide, we really oughta decide that tonight so I can make some calls," I said. "Do you have any interest, Becky, if we go?"

"Fishing?"

"Yeah. If we go with a guide, it will be on a flats boat. If we don't go with a guide, we'll get some advice and just find a shallow flat to fish at low tide."

"I like fishing about as much as Louie likes quilting," she replied. He gave a slight shake of the head as though he didn't want her to notice. Maybe a touchy subject.

I stood to go check on the fire, picking up my phone from the coffee table.

"See if you can bring up Barometer Bob there and check on the tides for this week," I said to Louie, dropping the phone into his lap.

He put his beer down, took the phone and looked at it. After studying it for a second, he swiped the screen, tapped one of the icons and began typing.

"Barometer Bob. Is that it?" he asked, watching the screen.

"Oughta come up. I found it this morning."

"Huh. Look at that. BarometerBob.org. Cool."

Fourteen
The Mud

Drink, dance, more. Depends on who you know. Joey knew one man with whom he held just enough trust that he would go with him to an illegal club reputed to have drinking and dancing. And it had. But not now, not tonight. Maybe another time.

Stanley was the man's name. He had shown Joey a handmade poster advertising "Music – Ladies Drink Free" scrawled with different colored markers. The poster also advertised "In da Mud." But Joey's recent activities might now preclude any drop-in visits to The Mud.

What neither Joey, nor Stanley, or the hundreds of residents knew, was that the Bahamian Department of Environmental Health Services was also aware of private, unlicensed, unsanitary 'clubs'. The DEHS folks had, in fact, produced an extensive report compiled from numerous on-site visits, with photos, documenting the deplorable conditions of shanty towns on four of the islands in the Bahamas: Eluthera, Andros, Exuma and Abaco.

The report included observations that the average dwelling was approximately *eighty square feet* and houses a family of six. And that while overcrowding was an issue, it was not as significant as the structural integrity concerns, along with minimal sewage, water infrastructure and solid waste management issues.

Profitable businesses varying in nature do exist in The Mud, the report said, including some liquor stores and convenience shops, numbers gambling, animal rearing - chickens, sheep, goats and pigs - cock fighting, recycling of bottles, and coal production.

Good Haitians, bad Haitians, squalid living conditions, these did not concern Joey. Earthquakes and hurricanes, not his problem, mon. He just wasn't civic minded. Looking now at his phone every few seconds, pacing back and forth in the tiny apartment, Joey was concerned with one thing; the resounding and repetitive soundtrack that he heard was ... leave, leave, leave.

The battery on his phone was running low. He couldn't find the plug for recharging. Did Atty take it? He threw clothes around and knocked items from the kitchen table. No sign of the charger. He would have to buy a new one. There was a store a few blocks away that sold them. Go right now and get one. Benji's son might call and his phone would be dead.

Joey went down the steps two at a time. Was the store still open? Since coming back from TC two days earlier, he avoided driving the pick-up. Much of his time in years past had been spent walking and downtown Marsh Harbour was not that big. He moved quickly, thoughts shifting to Stanley's story about 'nobody in da Mud' caring for the two men who'd been shot.

His phone rang. He stopped and looked at the screen. Not a number that he knew. After one more ring, he put the phone to his ear.

"Hello."

"Is this Joey," a woman's voice asked.

He hesitated, then said, "Yes. I am Joey. Who is dis?"

The connection was silent for a couple seconds, then the woman spoke again.

"Joey. Do you know me, Mirella Williams? I am Atty's sister, you remember?" Of course he remembered. He'd seen her for most of his adult life and when he and Atty were in school, long before the recent renewal of their acquaintance.

"Yes. I know you," he said.

"And you know my husband, Terrence?"

Everyone in Marsh Harbour and all the way down to Cherokee Sound knew Terrence Williams. Probably all of the other islands, too. Joey pictured the big man's smiling face in newspaper ads and the posters advertising his guide service.

"We do not want you spendin' no more time with Atty. What you do, where you go, dat is your business. Do not include my brother, hear me?"

He could hear her voice and her words, but it was the image of her *husband* that fully occupied Joey's mind.

Mirella abruptly broke the connection and placed the phone back inside her handbag. She took a deep breath, waited a second, then started the car to drive home.

Earlier in the day, while Atty had been asleep in her living room, Mirella had gone through the recent calls on his phone. She also found a number for Joey in the contacts list. She knew that Terrence would not hesitate to go to the police. It was her hope that a phone call would do the trick, that it would frighten Joey enough that he would stay away from Atty.

Forty-minutes later, much to her relief, when Mirella arrived home she found Atty watching TV with the volume turned low so that he would not to disturb Terrence sleeping in the next room. She plopped herself down on the sofa next to Atty.

"Did you eat?" she asked, patting his arm. He kept his eyes on the TV and shook his head. He pointed at the table in front of the sofa which held a nearly empty can of Bahamas Goombay Punch, the popular non-alcoholic soft drink version. There was also an empty pretzel bag.

"Maybe Terrence leave us some conch," she said, rising from the sofa and moving toward the refrigerator. She pulled out a large plastic bowl covered with a lid which she removed and studied the contents. Reaching into a cupboard next to the refrigerator, she took out two plates, got some utensils from a drawer and scooped portions of conch salad onto each plate.

The One Stop Shop in the Murphy Town section of Marsh Harbour had everything and Joey got there before it closed. It had the generic USB charger that would fit his phone. He paid for it and walked back to the apartment, plugged in the phone and opened a can of beer.

Sunday night, late. Joey's thinking hadn't changed. Still too late to go to The Mud if you didn't live there. But he would go find Stanley in the morning.

He thought more about it. We be knowin' more what da people are sayin' about da two men. Who shoot dem boys? Do dem boys have friends be comin' from Haiti?

His fear was not just of the RBPF locating him, but also his haste in dealing with the bad guys, which might have placed him in the sights of smarter, more resourceful characters coming from away. Leave before they find him.

Fifteen
Chill Out

Travelling can make you tired. Sunday night, not long after dinner, Becky Ragsdale was ready to get some rest. Louie and I stayed up talking a while longer and trying to agree on the best plan for fishing. And I was successful in booking a guide for Tuesday to take us out in his boat.

Over coffee and breakfast at Café La Florence Monday morning, Becky made the case for just hanging out at the beach for much of the day. Reading, walking, maybe gathering some shells and not thinking about rain, gray skies and cold temperatures back home.

So that's what we were doing. No radios, I hadn't heard one at the beach since I got here. No cell phones, at least not where we were stretched out. Nobody paddling or swimming out into the surf or doing anything that might draw attention. Just the warm breeze, the sun, the white sand and that amazing water as far as we could see.

"I can't believe the color," Becky said. "I've never seen anything like it. Not even the TV commercials and the web photos."

"I don't think they shoot any commercials here. Maybe, but I hope not. Let everybody go to Grand Bahama or Paradise Island," I said.

Louie was scouting the beach and the islands farther away through binoculars. I don't think he'd said a word since we pulled three chaise lounges out onto the beach. After a couple minutes, he let the binoculars hang from his neck, folded his hands across his stomach and looked at me.

"Whaddya know about crime here?" he asked. "Your friend give you any pointers about places to avoid?"

"Not specifically, no places that he told me about on Abaco. They do have some burglary, so you can't be stupid. Lock-up when you go out." As I answered this, I was pretty sure that Ragsdale had done some research before they came down.

"Of course, this beach compound," I extended my arm back toward the cottages behind us, "it's not really a gated community, but they have cameras and it's monitored. I don't think, like some places back in the states, I don't think there's a video feed connected to the local police station."

"I did some reading online," Louie said.

"Why am I not surprised?"

He shrugged when I said this. "Far as I can tell," he went on, "at least from an official annual report from the Royal Bahamas Police Commissioner, very similar drug problems to what we have in the states. Much of the serious crime, certainly major theft and murders, is related to drugs. Steal it, sell it, get cash, buy drugs."

"What'd the report say about violent crime, as compared to cities back home?" I asked.

Becky had started to get up for a walk, but now sat on the edge of her chaise listening to us.

"In 2014, they had a total of one-hundred-twenty-three murders, most of them on New Providence Island. That was an increase of three per cent over the year before," Louie said.

"One-hundred-twenty-three murders out of a total population of say... what, four-hundred-thousand people? How's that stack-up?"

Louie shook his head. "Apples and oranges. You can't compare it, say to Detroit, Chicago, even Baltimore. All those places have a population density that won't fit with the Bahamas. There's nobody *here*. How many people on this island?"

"I think Bill told me about thirteen-thousand for the whole island. About seven-hundred-seventy square miles."

"Right," Louie responded. "Think about that. You know how sparse the population is in northern New England. So, thirteen-thousand people *here* is like, maybe, *seventeen* per square mile! Even a tiny state like Vermont has more than sixty people per square mile."

"So, Captain," a rank I'd pinned on Louie shortly after we'd met during a kidnapping case in Maine a couple of years back, "whatd'ya have for stats on the murders in the

Bahamas, that one-hundred-twenty-three count?"

"Two thirds of the country's population live on two islands; New Providence, Nassau is the hub, connected to Paradise Island, and on Grand Bahama. *Combined* they had one-hundred-eighteen of those murders. That was two years ago."

"Whoah,' Becky piped up. "Let's stay right here, thank you." Louie looked at her and gave her the thumb-up, pointed index finger gesture that he frequently used on me.

"OK, I'm going for a walk," she added, getting up again. "Wanna come?"

"Can't wait," Louie said, taking off the binoculars and handing them to me. "How about you, Hanlon? Or, would you rather stay here and watch the scenery." He jerked his head in the direction of two women who had arrived a few minutes ago and were getting their umbrella and beach chairs set up. Nice bathing suits.

"Nah. I'll come along." I pushed myself up and put the binoculars back in the case with our towels, books and sunblock. I pointed down the beach to our right, beyond a little beach bar and food place called Coconuts.

"Let's go that way. Checkout some of those high end houses right at the point. Probably friends of Dick Cheney. Or maybe Trump."

Sixteen
Teams

Inspector Cynthia Knowles had completed a run of more than eight kilometers, showered and finished a light breakfast of yogurt, fruit and black coffee. Not all fellow officers still bothered with running. It was something she actually enjoyed from her days as a basketball player at SC Bootle High School in Cooper's Town.

She'd been the first one to enter the classroom arranged for the training sessions. Now, an hour later, after a short orientation and review of the schedule for the next five days, the small group of RBPF officers were paired-off into five teams and were taking a short break before the first lecture/Q & A coming up at 11 o'clock.

She had known in advance the list of names of the other officers who would be attending and had spoken with each of them when they arrived the previous day. But with everyone assembled here in a classroom, she was more keenly aware of being the only woman in the group. At least there was one other woman scheduled to give a presentation on Wednesday, Assistant Superintendent Stephanie Harris would be there to give the group an overview for a new media awareness campaign aimed at taking illegal firearms out of the communities around the Bahamas.

Knowles was matched with Inspector Denny Ring, currently assigned to the RBPF on Eleuthera. They would be known as Team Conch for the rest of the week. The four others were: Teams Callaloo, Coconut, Bonefish and Pineapple. Other than the RPBF Assistant Commissioner charged with overseeing and evaluating the participants, no one was quite sure how the names had been selected and, for that matter, how they would be scored in each activity. That had yet to be explained.

"Maybe Junkanoo dancing for most points," Denny Ring said.

"Will you wear a costume?" Knowles responded. He laughed and shook his head. Growing up, both had seen many carnival dances and the elaborate costumes at different Junkanoo Festivals held each year around the islands.

"We could get tee shirts made with our photo. RBPF Conch Team." Ring shook his head again.

"Maybe a bad idea, unless you be thinkin' a new job somewhere far away."

They joined the others back in the conference room. Without anyone directing them to do so, each person found a seat next to his new partner.

Romey McIntosh and Mirella Williams sat at a table near the swimming pool at The Tipsy. Drinking strawberry kiwi lemonade, they were the only two on the patio on a very quiet Monday morning. It was Mirella's break and Romey had just arrived. Following their previous conversation, Romey wanted to offer some support for her friend.

"Can he get a job?" Romey asked. "How about the market in Marsh Harbour?" Mirella shook her head, put her lemonade on the table and twisted the plastic cap back on.

"There are times when Atty is like a ten-year-old," Mirella said. "After he left school, for a while, he was OK. Sometimes he would help Terrence, painting the boat and little things." She looked directly at Romey, paused, then continued.

"He was a helper for a contractor fixing up homes on Man 'O War Cay. He didn't make much money, but he stayed out of trouble. After a year, the contractor left the island. Atty really hasn't done anything since then."

Romey kept quiet. She knew that at this moment her friend needed an empathetic ear, not another person to jump in with still more quick advice.

They talked some about the resort and a rumor that it was about to be sold. They speculated on what if any changes might occur with new owners. Would some lose their jobs, would money be invested in badly needed repair and upgrades of the guest rooms?

"They will keep you, girl," Mirella said, reaching across

the table and patting Romey on the shoulder. "You are the best bartender in all the islands," she laughed. "*You* be the Bahama Mama for a long time yet."

Romey playfully pushed Mirealla's hand away.

Mirella stood and picked up her lemonade. She looked out at the marina where some tourists were doing chores on boats. Gulls swooped the surface of the water and some landed on the posts along the boardwalk.

"When is the last time you came to Pizza Night?" Romey asked. Looking down at her friend still seated at the table, Mirella raised her eyebrows.

"No, really. When?" Romey added.

"Maybe ten years."

"I don't believe it."

Mirella nodded. "It's true. TD, Junior stayed with a friend. Terrence did not want to come, but I made him anyway. We have not been since then. Long time."

"It has changed. Everyone comes now, families. The pizzas are better and the music is fun."

Mirella gave no response. She picked up her phone and took a couple steps back toward the main building. She had others to check on and her own work to do. Romey wasn't finished.

"The music is great and the new singer is very good. He knows all the popular songs for the last 50 years. And there is this little girl, you won't believe her. She comes every week with her parents and always dances with her dad. She is going to be something." She went on, "Bring

Atty if Terrence will not come with you," Romey added.

"We will see," Mirella said. "Bye." She gave a little wave and went back to work

Seventeen
No Answer

Joey parked across from the school and walked to The Mud. Before leaving his truck, he shoved his .38 Special into his waistband and let his shirt hang over it.

Standing next to the truck, holding his phone, Joey gave the appearance of someone with Tourette syndrome, shaking his phone back and forth in his left hand and staring at the screen. All day long now he'd been holding the phone and checking the screen every few seconds.

Battery charged, but no calls.

He had planned to go see Benji again and ask if he had given his son Joey's phone number. Instead, he decided first to come find Stanley. Of all the Haitian men Joey had met from The Mud, he never knew anyone's last name. He wasn't sure they knew his last name. It was always, "Joey, mon," or "Hey mon, Stanley." More often no name at all in their greetings, just a lazy high five, maybe, and "How you doin', mon?"

Amongst all the clutter, sewage, chickens running around, dogs, some goats and the battered shacks leaning against one another, Joey thought that he could find the place where Stanley hung out. It was the same place where they'd gone for the music and dancing, a bright blue house only slightly larger than the shanties. There had been two windows, one on either side of a front door that was painted pink.

Nobody spoke as he walked between the tight rows of shacks, but Joey was sure that some were watching him. He kept moving.

Three men were standing together fifty feet ahead. He could see the blue paint behind them and walked in that direction. As he got closer, one of the men, taller than even Joey, stopped talking and looked at him. The other two turned to look as well. One of the men was Stanley.

Atty was fidgety with absolutely nothing to do. No contact with Joey in three days and stuck with unwanted supervision from his sister. It was like he was back in school.

Mirella was at work and TD was at his girlfriend's house where he helped her father clean and maintain rental golf carts. Atty really didn't care for anything he saw on TV and he didn't like to read. After too much time inside, he was eager to go out.

Some of Atty's acquaintances from school days, at least those like him with no job, still hung around Marsh Harbour in the middle of the day. He knew a few guys would be down at the ferry dock hanging out. Others would go to the benches outside the market in the center of town. None of these guys were Atty's friends. Most had avoided him in school. That had not changed in the few years since.

He thought about the money Joey had promised and recalled the wad of cash he'd seen. He thought about Joey being his only friend. He knew Joey had made a lot of talk in the past about leaving Abaco. Often something like, 'I be gone from here, mon.' When, or to where, Joey never explained.

Pulling a shirt over his head, letting it hang out over his baggy pants, Atty put on his shoes and headed for the door.

Apprehending Haitians, or *any* other illegal migrants without work permits, was not uncommon for police in Marsh Harbour. If you listened to many native Bahamians, it was not common enough.

Resentment had lingered for years, even before the devastating 7.0 earthquake on Haiti in 2010 that took thousands of lives and sent still more Haitian survivors to other islands, as well as the more recent Hurricane Matthew that hit Haiti dead on, claiming hundreds of lives.

One reader's letter to *The Nassau Guardian* offered this view: 'The Marsh Harbour Softball Field is no more and hundreds of shanty houses crowd the area with very little room left for vehicles to get through. PVC pipes, illegally set up, run across roads and provide limited running water to houses that are put together with scrap wood and definitely not up to code. Illegal immigrants land on the shores every few weeks (especially with the full moon) and in broad daylight they build homes on property that does not belong to them.'

Like other rough neighborhoods all over the world, The Mud had its share of crime, ranging from assault incidents committed against residents, to armed robbery and a murder in a nearby convenience store a few years back.

Depending on your source of information regarding the current situation, there was one perception that local government's efforts to deal with the issue was too often hampered by a real lack of support at the federal level.

Regardless of the incredible poverty in Haiti, you will find in the Bahamas, frustration and strong opinions on both sides of the immigration issue just one conversation away.

Eighteen
Patchwork

A salad of tomatoes, cucumbers and red onion, fresh bread from the bakery and more grilled fish. Is there a Bahamian diet we don't know about back in the states?

Becky made the salad and sliced the bread. I grilled the dolphin fish. Louie took charge of the music, spending way too much time going through a shelf of CDs. Our dinner entertainment was pretty good, though: a DJ Sampler of *Old School Bahamian*, a duo collection with Sweet Emily and Ronnie Butler, and Phil Stubb's *Bonefish Folley*.

After cleaning up and putting the dishes away, all three of us talked about the recent US Presidential election and what the media spin would be like over the next few weeks. We were in total agreement that it would be refreshing not to have to see the ads and hear the bombardment on radio. Then I told Becky and Louie a little of what I'd read about the politics in the Bahamas.

"Like the US, they have two major parties. Here it's

the Progressive Liberal Party, the PLP, and the Free National Movement, or FNM. The PLP is currently on top. Their next election is coming up in May. They vote every *five* years. And," I paused for effect, "get this. They have a voter turnout that averages more than ninety per cent!"

"When did the Bahamas become a nation?" Becky asked.

"Prince Charles delivered the documents himself after the House of Lords voted to grant independence. July 10th, 1973."

"Wow. Not that long ago. I was in the third grade," Becky replied.

"And I was already studying music on *WACE*, 730 on your AM dial," Louie added.

"Here we go," I said. "And do tell us, Brother Ragsdale, what great hits from 1973 most influenced your musical taste today?"

Becky and I both watched. Louie closed his eyes and held a hand to his forehead like he was psychic, then opened his eyes and gave us a smug look.

"O'Jays. *Love Train*."

"Tell all the folks in Russia and China, too," I said.

"You got it. Very good, Hanlon. Classic stuff," he replied. Becky had heard and seen this show one too many times. She got up to get ready for bed.

"Don't stay up too late. What time is the guide picking you up?" she asked.

"Eight. We need to have our gear out front and bring

sandwiches and something to drink," I said.

Ragsdale and I were looking at bonefish flies and checking tippet material five minutes later when Becky came back to the living room. She was carrying a large coffee table book, which she handed to me. *Gee's Bend – The Women and Their Quilts*.

"You should look at this, Michael. It's a pretty amazing story. I saw these quilts a few years ago at the Chrysler Museum in Norfolk, Virginia. I was visiting a college friend. Some of the quilt makers were there and talked about their work."

"Must've added some weight to your luggage," I said, hefting the book.

"It was under the nightstand," she said, pointing back toward the bedroom. "I have a copy at home. Some really beautiful quilts."

"Right up your alley, Hanlon," Louie said, getting up to join his wife. He tapped me on top of the head. "Don't stay up too late."

Having grown up with quilts made by my grandmother I'd seen a few impressive works that she produced, sometimes alone and occasionally in collaboration with a friend. When I visited her house as a kid, colorful pieces of fabric and other sewing stuff was always lying around somewhere. My mother told me that when she was little, Granma made clothing from old feed bags.

So, with just a twinge of guilt about my relatively

easy life and off-the-rack clothing, along with fond memories of my grandmother, I put the fly box back in my tackle bag and waded into the quilt book.

Full page color plates of the quilts, some going back nearly a hundred years, along with photos and interviews with the quilt makers and stories of their ancestors. Some of the women were descendants of the same young slave, a woman known as Dinah, brought to a plantation in Alabama before the Civil War.

Flipping through the book I found myself reading more about the women and their relatives than actually looking at the quilt patterns. Great names: Ma Willie Abrams, Indiana Bendolph Pettway, Arlonzia Pettway. And the photos of these women. Somebody really knew how to take outstanding portraits.

It was near midnight before I put the book down. Getting ready for bed I thought about the images of the quilts, not unlike some landscape patterns you see when you're in an airplane. Or one of those tricky digital art works in a photograph of a large mass of people, with an array of colors that could almost fool you into thinking the photo was staged.

Something else occurred to me. The vibrant colors I'd observed after only a few days on Abaco were just a tad different from back home. Vermont has lush green hills and valleys in the summer, the fall foliage can be really vibrant and even the vast whiteness of a good winter is nice to see. But there's a lot to appreciate in the colors and culture of other people and places.

Aside from being just another tourist, I wondered what the Bahamians thought of us.

Nineteen
12 o'clock/Strip!

The plan was that Becky was going to rent a bicycle and spend the day exploring Treasure Cay while Louie and I were out fishing.

"Remember, it's a little different than a spinning bike at the gym," Ragsdale said to his wife as we walked out the door. She kissed him on the cheek and patted his back.

"Have fun," she said.

Our guide, Leevan Clarke, apparently known far and wide simply as "LC", stood waiting next to his white GMC pick-up with a flats boat on a trailer hooked behind. Wearing khaki shorts, a long-sleeved shirt, sandals, wrap-around sunglasses and a wide-brim hat, he looked to be six-feet and maybe a hundred-seventy-five pounds. He had a big smile as he extended his hand to greet us.

"Good morning," he said with a deep, Bahamian lilt. He shook our hands as we introduced ourselves, took our gear and placed it in the back of the truck and we headed out for a ten-minute drive to the western side of the island and a place known as The Marls.

I yapped at him most of the way explaining that while both Louie and I had considerable experience in fresh water fishing and for striped bass along the New England coast, neither of us had ever been bone fishing and we were counting on him.

"No worry, mon. We will get some fish," he offered, turning onto a dirt road just off the main highway. Not a minute later, he was backing the trailer down to a small wooden boat dock tucked in a narrow opening of mangroves at the edge of the water.

The boat looked to be twenty feet or more, had a vinyl-padded bench seat in front of a center console and a raised platform in the stern just above the motor. I knew from reading and photos that the guides stood on the platform to spot fish and pole the boat forward without using the motor. The boat was spotless and could have just come from the manufacturer. We transferred our gear, held the line while LC parked the truck and trailer, then pushed off.

Slowly maneuvering through mangroves we emerged into open water and moved along close to shore for a couple minutes. LC killed the motor and got up onto the platform. Louie and I were obedient sports, sitting quietly and waiting for instruction.

With a slim graphite pole, maybe fifteen feet in length and not two inches in diameter, LC slowly and quietly pushed the boat ahead in water only three or four feet deep. We could see dark red starfish resting on the bottom, sprawling mangroves along the shore and in scattered clumps across the water. After a minute, LC stopped using the pole and whispered, "Dare. By da mangrove." He was pointing with his right arm to a spot more than sixty feet away. I saw nothing but water and the spider-like branches and leaves of the mangroves rising off the surface.

Louie didn't say anything, so I was guessing that he saw what I saw; zip. LC smoothly moved the pole again in a quiet, long stroke and we moved in closer.

"See da fins," he said, voice just loud enough for us to hear.

Still nothing. Then, like some translucent butterflies that had just suddenly appeared, I saw a glistening movement on the surface. It was a very slow, circular motion.

"They're tailing," Louie said, also near whispering.

"Yes," LC said. "Find da shrimp."

We'd read about it. Bonefish feeding off the bottom, going nose down like a diving airplane with their tail fins protruding at the surface. In this case, more than one fish in the same spot and their fins moving around like ballet dancers.

"Be ready to throw da line," LC said. "Wait 'til we closer."

By lunch time we'd caught and released three bonefish. Louie had two, I had one. And we had missed two other fish.

LC instructed us to stand, barefoot, near the bow and to remember that regardless of how we positioned our feet that the direction of 12 o'clock was *always* the bow. He would tell us when he spotted fish, '20 feet at 10 o'clock,' or, 'Two fish coming, 40 feet, 1 o'clock' and so on. It took a while to catch on.

The most popular fly pattern looked like a tiny shrimp. We would try to cast the fly in front of the fish, let it sink, then retrieve line, fast or slow depending on what LC told us, hoping the fish would take. When it did, if you could set the hook properly, even small fish could strip out most of your line and maybe make a couple of good runs before being brought to the boat, then released.

The Marls opened into a vast expanse, and looking across the water gave me a real sense of why early explorers could have believed the earth was flat. You could just sail out there and drop right off.

Leevan Clarke was a good guide. And patient. One frustratiing moment came when I missed a fish. As I stood on the bow gazing at the distance, LC suddenly said, "12 o'clock, big fish. 30 feet. Cast now." I put out some line, let the fly drop and waited.

"Strip, strip. Wait. *Strip!*" he said. Then, "Ahh, mon. Gone." That fish was moving on.

Before the afternoon was over, we had two more fish.

I caught one that might've gone five pounds. Louie hooked a beauty that LC said was big for The Marls, probably seven pounds.

Driving back, we talked about other places to fish and other guides, some from before LC was born. I guessed him to be in his mid-forties. He said that he'd been guiding for over twenty years.

"You want da big fish," LC said "you go wit Cap'n Rick over on Green Turtle. Or, maybe Ronnie or Jeff take you to Cooper's Town. I just fish da Marls, sometimes down to Sandy Point."

Some earlier reading and looking at maps had shown us that Green Turtle Cay was not far away, that Cooper's Town was to the north and Sandy Point to the south of the island.

We made a quick stop on the way back to the cottage. While standing at the checkout in a wine and liquor store, we watched in amusement as a small Bahamian man waltzed in, shoulders moving to some music in his ear buds and arms waving slowly like a gliding seagull. The guy wore a multi-colored knit hat, a bright yellow shirt, ragged old blue jeans and scuffed work boots.

"Gimme all of da rum ……… and all of da Coke," he declared as though he was singing it.

Apparently the man was well-known to the clerk, who in a low key reply hit it out of the park.

"Whatever you say, mon," he said, not taking his eyes from the register. The little guy proceeded to a cooler, pulled out a six pack of beer and got in line behind us, head moving and still swaying to the sounds only he could hear.

Arriving back at the cottage, we paid LC. Normal fee for full-day guided fishing for two was $450. We tipped him another $80. He was happy, we were happy. Louie and I now had a new fishing experience to analyze and embellish.

After hosing the saltwater off our gear and getting cleaned up, we had a beer, chips and salsa on the patio, and gave Becky a brief rundown of the day's events. Then I milked the story of the first sighting of the bonefish tailing and how it made me think of ballet. She seemed to buy it.

Tomorrow would be Wednesday. Becky had arranged for snorkeling lessons and Louie was being the good husband, pretending to be pleased about going along.

I excused myself for a few minutes, took my phone and walked over to the beach to call Romey McIntosh.

Twenty
New Mon

Stanley repeated to Joey a story that the men who had been shot were part of a smuggling ring believed to be moving drugs all over the Bahamas. Joey already knew some of this. Another part of this story was that the men first showed up here shortly after Hurricane Matthew.

Stanley then told him that another man, reportedly from Port-au-Prince, had come to Abaco, visited The Mud and was an acquaintance of the two who had been shot. This other man was believed still to be on the island.

"He be here two days ago," Stanley said.

"How do you know he is still here?" Stanley shrugged and raised his hands palms up.

"It is what I am told."

This was new information to Joey, part of the reason for this particular visit to The Mud. Better to get the gossip from Stanley than learn about it from the police.

"Where is dis man?"

Stanley didn't reply, but his eyes shifted to the left, in the same direction where the men he'd been talking with had gone. Joey looked that way. The men were now out of view. Joey jerked his head in that direction.

"Dem boys know dis man? What is his name?"

"I hear his friend call him Jameson," said Stanley.

"Dose men your friends?"

"I know one of dem for long time now. Since I come to Abaco."

"I would like to meet dis man from Port-au-Prince," Joey said.

"Maybe come back tonight. I will be talking with my friend." Stanley turned to leave.

Joey stood in place, not moving for a few seconds as he watched Stanley walk away. There was music coming from a radio inside the blue building.

When Joey stuck his head inside the door he saw an old man sitting on a stool at the far end of the room. The man was working on something inside a small box on a counter. The man gave no attention to Joey.

Taking the phone out of his back pocket as he left The Mud, Joey resumed the close-in, hand-to-hand juggling of the device and looking at the screen. No indication of any calls. He walked across the street to his truck.

Atty couldn't find Joey. The pick-up was not in its usual parking spot behind the apartment building where Joey lived. Maybe he'd actually left the island.

Using a ballpoint pen and scribbling on a piece of

paper from his pocket, Atty wrote a note and shoved it under Joey's door.

I WANT TO GO. ATTY.

If Joey were still here, Atty hoped they would connect. Even though some of Joey's recent behavior had scared him, the apprehension caused by thinking of his brother-in-law Terrence and the possibility of Atty having to face the police alone was more frightening.

Going back through the center of town, watching cars and constantly glancing in all directions as he walked, Atty wrestled with conflicting thoughts of all the hovering concern that he got from his sister against a gnawing curiosity about a life not here on Abaco. Joey was the only person whom Atty believed could help him.

Up ahead at a stop sign, Atty spotted Joey's truck. It was coming in his direction. He waited on the corner and raised both hands to wave for Joey.

The frequency and frustration of boat thefts had become nearly an epidemic in the Northern Bahamas. More recently, however, police had made progress in both finding the boats and actually making arrests. It was one of the top priorities for the RBPF.

One recent incident was an early morning capture of three young men in a boat off Elbow Cay. And *that* was followed just a week later by the arrest of the two men who'd been shot and the actual recovery of a boat in their possession. They were found on a beach to the south and the boat was traced to a non-resident owner who kept a slip in the Marsh Harbour Marina.

One of the men had died from his wounds two days later and the other one was not cooperating with police. He was sent to Nassau for processing and would either be imprisoned there or deported back to Haiti.

It was not uncommon for drug runners to be intercepted in cooperative efforts that involved the RPBF Marine Support Service and the US Coast Guard. But islands like Abaco had limited resources and there were numerous places where boats could slip in and out avoiding detection.

Most drugs seized by authorities were at the country's largest airport, Lynden Pindling International in Nassau. Many of the passengers detained were attempting to go on to the US. Then there were all of the drugs *not seized* or consumed in the islands.

While much of the public all over the western hemisphere might see a story about refugees packed onto boats that went aground or capsized, stories reporting the interdiction of drug smugglers and the seizure of their illegal cargo rarely captured the media's attention.

A couple guys and a stolen boat on a Bahamian island were not going to make CNN.

Twenty One
Listen Up

Clear eyes, scrubbed faces, clean ears. There was no 'Class Monitor' checking fingernails and making sure that everyone had a clean handkerchief, but ten alert RBPF officers came to attention when the morning session got underway.

"Do you know her?" Denny Ring asked. Cynthia Knowles nodded.

"She is new with Public Affairs and Communications," Knowles whispered.

The figure at the front of the room, all five-feet, eight inches of a fit, handsome, no-nonsense woman in a her crisp RBPF uniform – light blue shirt over a navy skirt – gazed out at the police officers seated at the classroom tables.

The badges of Assistant Superintendent on her epaulets, reading glasses on a simple black leather cord around her neck, she waited until the room was completely silent. With both arms raised to shoulder height, she extended her hands as though she were trying to stop an onrushing crowd. Fingers spread, she held the hands in place for effect and waited a beat before speaking.

"The prevention and detection of crime." She folded her right thumb inward. "Reducing the fear of crime." Right index finger folded over the thumb. Her voice was clear, with diction and pacing that held their attention.

"Restoring and maintaining public trust and confidence. The safety and security of the public. Working with young people. The protection of the tourist industry. And the efficient management of resources."

As she ticked off each of these, another finger was folded into her hand until only the last three fingers on her left hand remained erect, giving the appearance of someone indicating the 'OK' sign. She held that sign as she walked from behind the podium and moved about the tables.

"We all know the strategic priorities. We learned them when we were young recruits and we've heard them on more than one occasion from the Commissioner."

She dropped the left arm, clasped her hands together and lowered them to her stomach as if she might be hiding jelly beans or a piece of candy. Then she walked to a window looking out onto the water not a hundred feet from the building.

"I have three other points that I would like us to consider this morning." She returned to the podium, her back to the audience and left arm raised as she walked, making the 'OK' sign again with three fingers up.

Facing the RBPF rising stars seated in front of her, the woman smiled for the first time.

"Good morning. I am ASP Stephanie Harris. I know most of you and am honored to be part of today's discussion."

"Each of you was selected to be part of this pilot training program *not* just because of what you have accomplished during your time on the force. Each of you," she paused, slowly scanning the faces, "are part of a crucial link for everything we do from this date forward. Which brings me to what I would like us to focus on for the rest of the day, this morning and continuing with our session after lunch."

The session was not being recorded and there were no cameras. Had there been, someone watching later might have noticed that almost as though a signal went out, everyone seated at the tables seemed to relax in sync with the speaker's measured and confident delivery.

Left arm back up, the OK sign and the three extended fingers.

"Tomorrow," middle finger folded down. "The next day," ring finger down, just her pinky still up as she rotated her wrist and made the finger move back and forth.

"And every day after that." She used the little finger now as an imaginary symbol held above her head.

"For the rest of your career with the Royal Bahamas Police Force, possibly for the rest of your life, what you do with those strategic priorities and all of the challenges ahead, will make the difference between how our country is viewed today, not yet three generations independent, and how we are viewed by generations still to come."

ASP Harris folded her arms, leaned forward on the podium and waited. Everyone had a dark blue, three-ring binder on the table in front of him. Harris had the same binder resting in front of her.

"We'll see a video in a few minutes. But first, let's go to the green tab in the folder that reads Day Three – Communication."

A fifteen-minute drive south of Cooper's Town, away from the RBPF training session, was a dirt road that lead to a recently failed fruit and vegetable farm with a few small buildings. Past the farm, a little farther into the pine forest, not easily visible unless you were looking for it, was a deep marine cavern known as a blue hole.

Containing both fresh and saltwater, this blue hole is one of possibly a thousand discovered around the Bahamas. Serious exploration has been underway in the last twenty years and has a lot of scientists and marine biologists pretty excited, not to mention divers and underwater photographers. Most of the holes are in the sea and most are on or near Andros, the larger island to the south. This particular spot is one of only a few *inland* holes on Great Abaco.

Twenty Two
Deep

"Does it have a name?" I asked. "All the blue holes I read about seem to have names. Dan's Cave, Sawmill Sink, Dean's Blue Hole."

"We call it Treasure Cay blue hole," Romey said. "That is all that I have ever heard since I was a child."

Maybe fifty feet or more in diameter, the hole was surrounded by rocks, shrub growth and tall pine trees. Other than that, it looked similar to a small livestock pond that you might expect to see on a farm. Except for the *color*.

The surface was clear, not quite the blue off the Treasure Cay beach. Then perhaps twenty feet down it became cloudy, like it had been recently stirred up. Around the edge of the water it was apparent that the area had occasional human foot traffic on the path.

We walked closer and stood on a flat rock about two feet from the edge.

"One of the articles I read said the deepest blue hole ever discovered goes down over twelve-hundred feet. I think it's in Italy. Any idea how deep this is?" I asked.

107

Romey shook her head, bent slightly at the waist and peered into the water.

"My father told us that it went to the bottom of the sea. There have been divers and scientists doing research here. And on other islands," she said, waving an arm.

We walked completely around the pond, getting different angles to try to see the depth. I resisted a temptation to drop a pebble to see how far it would sink. After a few minutes we moved back in the direction of the car. I had the thought that some previous visitors probably dropped coins and made a wish. That provoked an imaginary reaction from a future archeological diver, 'Look at this. A 1986 Silver American Eagle coin.' Then maybe not.

"The article I read in *National Geographic* had a photo of a three-thousand-year-old Cuban crocodile skull. Divers found it in one of holes on Andros," I said.

Romey stopped and turned to face me. "How do they know it was Cuban?"

"I think it was of a species they've traced that still exists there."

"Hmm." She nodded and continued walking.

"Maybe they found a baseball in its jaw. Or old cigars."

Romey gave me a look over her shoulder.

"Humor," I said.

"Oh."

When we got to the car, she opened the driver's door.

I'd started for that side of the car when I remembered that the steering was on the right. She smiled and got behind the wheel, I went around to my seat on the left.

Driving back to the highway, she turned in the opposite direction from the way we came in, going left and out past the airport away from Treasure Cay.

When we'd spoken on the phone last night, Romey not only offered to drive me to see the blue hole, but said that she would take me all the way to the tip of the island, a few miles beyond the small village where she grew up. My contribution was that I brought along sandwiches, fruit, cookies and a couple of bottles of water.

The drive reminded me of rural highways I'd travelled in the US south. Long stretches of pine trees and undergrowth, but no branches near the ground. And at a couple different spots along the road, resting on utility poles, pairs and groups of turkey vultures.

"Waiting for a meal," I said.

Romey glanced at one pair of vultures. "The female is the one on the right," she said.

"Really? How can you tell?"

"She is larger."

"Are you making that up?" I turned my head to watch the birds as we passed. She laughed and shook her head.

"I am not making that up. We learn that as school children."

She slowed driving through Cooper's Town, pointing out different landmarks and homes, the school, a church.

"Hubert Ingraham still has a home here," she said, pointing at a street ahead.

"The former Prime Minister," I said. I'd also read about him, the guy who had been their PM in three different terms for a total of fifteen years, more than a third of their time as an independent country.

"Yes."

"Do you know him?" I asked. She laughed again.

"All on Abaco know Hubert. He is a good man."

The road made a distinct, ninety degree left turn. I assumed that we were now heading west. Romey kept her speed limit at about thirty.

"This is Little Abaco," she said as we crossed a bridge. "Where the islands connect."

No real change, other than the road became more narrow and we could see the water in all directions. I knew from looking at maps and photos that there were only a couple of even smaller villages beyond this point and then the highway ended. If you wanted to go to any of the small outer islands, get on a boat.

Romey turned the car around, pulled over and we got out. She pointed back in the direction where we'd been and would return.

"Out there is Spanish Cay. It also has a small airfield." She turned to face me and pointed over my shoulder. "Over there is Grand Bahama."

I looked in that direction, then raised my right arm and pointed north.

"Out there, somewhere, is Walker's Cay," I said.

"You know this how?"

"Hot spot for wealthy fishermen. There was an American cable TV show a few years ago that filmed there. I think it really gets hammered with hurricanes when they come through here."

"Just last month. And it was about this time four years ago, no, earlier. The end of October. That was Hurricane Sandy. We had no power for a long time," Romey said.

I didn't know what happened with Hurricane Matthew. Still looking off to where I imagined Walker's Cay to be, thinking about the old TV show and what the place might look like now, I tried to imagine how such storms impacted the fishing.

We stood for a minute taking in a full 360 view. On the road directly ahead of us was a man with a really old bicycle. He'd stopped and was doing something with one of the tires. We watched him for a minute, then I turned to Romey.

"Wanna' have some lunch?" I asked.

"Yes. There is a place where we can stop in Cooper's Town."

Twenty Three
Get A Job

Joey had waited in his truck. He believed that Atty was not coming. Phone in his lap, he distractedly fiddled with the starfish coin on the gold chain he wore around his neck.

Boredom, petty burglary, unchecked testosterone, not much love. If a child psychologist had been on the scene compiling a weekly journal of Joey's early development and adolescence, those words would have regularly found their way into the narrative.

Tall at a very young age, quick to respond to negative encouragement and to act out in almost any situation, particularly in school, Joey seemed to have slipped into a bad groove before he reached puberty. And like one of those little toy cars that race around a track, the more time Joey spent in his slot, the faster he went. And it only got worse in his late teens.

Unwilling to finish school and unable to find emotional stability of any kind, Joey began honing a trait that he most likely inherited from the long-gone father that he never knew. The clownishness and acting out from the teen years were now developing into a mean spirited disregard for just about everyone who came near him. The exception was a friend whom he could cajole and intimidate.

Now, at the ripe age of twenty-five, a taste for violence had seeped into Joey's demeanor. Shooting two men over a disagreement about payment for a stolen boat was the first time he had used a firearm in one of his crimes.

It would be only a matter of time before Joey was apprehended for one thing or another. He knew that. The island was too small. Everyone knew someone, or was related to someone who almost certainly knew Joey. He needed to leave, go to Grand Bahama or Nassau. That thought was now guiding everything he did. Leave now, before it's too late. Before he was connected to the shooting of the two men, one of whom had died a few days after his arrest.

Joey's immediate problem, besides needing more cash, was figuring out how to break away from Atty Gilbert. He knew that when he left that he would not take Atty with him.

Mirella asked Atty if he wanted to try find work at the resort in Treasure Cay. She sat in the plastic chair on the tiny deck at the back of the house. Atty stood, leaning against the open door to the kitchen. He stared at her and didn't answer. If she'd known about the recent close call that Joey and Atty had at the resort, *she* might call the police.

"They gonna have new owners soon," she said. "Some of dose men not gonna' be there, I tell you dat," she said. "You wanna keep a job, you have to *work*."

No response. Unlike all the chattering when he was around Joey, when he was in the presence of his sister, Atty dropped into a borderline trance, usually only reacting with shrugs, maybe a nod or shake of his head. It had been like this since childhood. Few words came out of him.

Ever since he had lost the job with the contractor, Mirella had thought that Atty was like one of the little geckos she often saw: frozen in place, staring up and ready to run off at any second.

Atty shifted his feet and looked out toward the street.

"You ride with me," she started again. "I talk to Emmett. They need boys who will help clean da fronds and coconuts. Keep the tennis court clean. Other tings like dat. You be dare on time, work hard. It is good for you."

Mirella got up from the chair. She stopped next to Atty, patted his cheek, then went into the house. As she rinsed her coffee cup, she kept talking.

"This afternoon I will speak with Emmet. He is boss of da buildings and grounds." Turning back to look at Atty, she had another idea.

"Romey wants me to come to Pizza Night. You remember, every Thursday in TC," she said. "Terrence will not be here. He has a fishing trip. You can go with me."

Stanley knew the Port-au-Prince man only by the name Jameson. Once he'd made the connection with the man for Joey, back to daily survival.

Even though the work was irregular and the pay was low, Stanley accepted the unpredictability of his life on Abaco. He would go to the docks, go to the center of town, go *anywhere* in Marsh Harbour if he thought that he could earn a few dollars.

Aware of other Haitians, like himself, who had legal work permits for the Bahamas but had later been deported, Stanley had no interest in being caught and charged with hiding illegal compatriots. He was relieved and not really surprised when the man Jameson seemed to be gone from The Mud as quickly as he had arrived.

After being surprised to see Atty on the street and stopping for him, Joey had made a second trip back to The Mud last night. The meeting Stanley had arranged with the man from Port-au-Prince had produced a new level of hope for Joey, alleviating some of his earlier fear.

It sounded as though the man was on Abaco to tie up loose ends, or to make sure that people who were doing things they shouldn't be doing, didn't talk about previous things they had done. Or, that they did not disclose the identity of former associates. The man said that he would reward' any help that Joey might be able to offer.

The exchange between the two prompted Joey to make a gamble. He agreed for the man to come to his apartment. And that's where they were at this moment.

But no matter what this man needed to do, Atty was Joey's loose end. But Atty was a 'no show'.

Some cash might do it. Scaring him wasn't likely to have much effect. Atty was born scared. Ever since their school days, Joey shared a view held by many that Atty was one nervous, moody young man. That came home in spades with the recent attempted robbery in TC.

Joey hadn't liked the phone call from Atty's sister. And he absolutely wanted nothing to do with her husband. But every time Atty came around, all of a sudden it seemed that he would turn into a 'parrot ass,' always talkin' about dis or dat. Now he wanted to go with Joey. Too much. Time to be still. But where is he?

Twenty Four
Cousins/Sisters

Like some enthusiastic tour guide from a cruise ship, Inspector Cytnthia Knowles led a few of her fellow officers on a short stroll to the Cooper's Town School.

After lunch, Inspector Denny Ring and four others accepted Knowles invitation for the quick tour. They wanted to stretch their legs. The four officers who'd been designated Team Callaloo and the Team Pineapple stayed behind.

"This is where you were the basketball star?" Ring asked.

"We had a good team. I was not the only one"

The group stopped briefly at the edge of the school parking lot, then turned to head back down the hill and back to their *own* classroom. Six people in police uniforms, out meandering in the middle of the afternoon in a small village. Hard to miss.

As they were about to cross the street, a passing car braked, stopped and pulled to the side of the road. The officers watched as a woman driver got out of the car.

"Well mudda sick," the woman said, standing next to

the car and laughing. Then Inspector Knowles started laughing, went to the driver and gave her a hug.

The somewhat puzzled RBPF officers watched the exchange. Inspector Denny Ring suspected that the woman was an old friend or relative of Knowles. He'd talked with her briefly about growing up in Cooper's Town.

After the two women had chatted for a minute, Knowles rejoined her colleagues and they returned to their afternoon training. Romey climbed back into the car, drove another five-hundred feet or so, then turned onto a short road that led from the highway to the water.

"Mudda sick?" Hanlon said. Romey looked at him, laughed and waved her arm like she was batting away an insect.

"What does it mean?"

"Dat is Cyndy. She is my cousin. More like my sister."

"Mudda sick means cousin? Sister?"

"No." Again the dismissive wave. "It is what we *say* when we are surprised." Hanlon let that sink in.

"So, I could say, 'It is *mudda sick* to see a bunch of policemen out walking around in the middle of the day? Like it's recess at the school?" She was shaking her head before he finished the question.

"Not like that," she responded. She glanced at him, still smiling, then went on with an explanation.

"I know this English woman. She come here every winter. Very nice older woman. She always be saying, 'Oh my,' when she is surprised to learn something."

118

Romey watched his reaction as she stopped the car. They had arrived at a small, sandy turn around area with enough room for one vehicle and just a few feet from the water's edge.

We sat staring at each other. It was obvious that she was doing her best not to laugh at me.

"You see it in a movie. Or read in a book, when someone is surprised to see something," Romey said. I thought about that.

"Like, *egad*. Or, yikes," I offered.

"Maybe. Like dat."

She opened the door and got out. I reached to the backseat for our lunch, an insulated bag containing two tomato/cucumber and cheese sandwiches, two nectarines, four oatmeal raisin cookies, some paper napkins and two bottles of water, then followed Romey.

A blue-green tropical print short sleeve shirt, pale yellow slacks that went to mid-calf, and open-toe sandals with cork soles. Sorry I didn't have a camera. And my phone was back at the cottage. On the other hand, even if we were to take a selfie, my khaki shorts, boring gray long-sleeve tee shirt with the redcrossblood.org logo, would bland out Romey's colors and beautiful skin. But then there was the smile. And her eyes.

We found a spot to sit on the rocks, not easy to do because of the volcanic crust-like nature of the shoreline. Romey watched as I spread a beach towel across the uneven surface and placed the food in the center of the towel.

"Please," I said, gesturing with my right hand as if I had just escorted her to the best table in a restaurant. She smiled, tilted her head and carefully found a way to settle on a rock, one leg stretched toward the water and the other folded back, placing her right foot under her left knee.

We unwrapped the sandwiches, ate slowly without much talk, and watched as an occasional boat appeared on the horizon. Then she pointed out Green Turtle Cay, clearly visible to the east, and told me about the island, including that Green Turtle had an annual Heritage Festival held over a three-day weekend in early May.

She explained that like Marsh Harbour and the smaller outlying cays to the south, there was a ferry service that made daily trips to and from Green Turtle.

"Year 'round?" I asked.

"Oh, yes. It is not just tourists. Many people who live on Abaco go there," she pointed in the direction of the smaller island, "to work. Everyday."

"Really?"

"*Real-ly*," she mimicked. "Restaurants. There is also a small resort. And private homes."

While we ate the nectarines and cookies, with a little prodding I got her to talk about her life on Abaco; family, work, her cousin Cyndy, the RBPF officer. I tried to softly peddle each question after the last answer. I could hear

Ragsdale's voice; 'Christ, Hanlon. You gonna' phone this in? Special vacation assignment for AP?'

It was something that I often would do without much forethought. When I met someone new, if we got into a conversation longer than two minutes, I would reflexively begin asking questions about that person's life, where they were from, family, their interests, slowly building a profile in my mind and pivoting to anything I thought we might have in common.

Experience had taught me, I think it might've come by way of advice from an old broadcasting mentor, to stay away from asking about political views. If they had 'em and were not shy, soon enough you were going to get the monologue.

After a few minutes, Romey turned it around. We had talked only superficially at the bar a couple of nights ago and I couldn't recall what I'd told her.

"How about your family?" she asked.

I plodded through, talking about parents deceased, my older sister who was a school teacher in California, cousins back in Pennsylvania, some aunts and uncles still living, ticking it off as if I was responding to a census taker's questions.

Then I waded through telling her about all my years in radio and the recent switch to this weird combination of media PR, security and private investigation work. Without gory details, I included just a little of the nasty stuff from the very first case I'd been involved with. My brain flashed on the wording of the phony business ad that Ragsdale had suggested I run. The pause gave Romey an opening.

"And you are not married?" she asked, showing mild surprise I thought . I shook my head.

"Divorced. Three years ago."

She didn't respond, just a slight nod, nothing judgmental.

"How about you," I said. Even though I'd previously learned that she was not presently attached to anyone, I took the opening. "Ever been married?"

She shook her head. "Never."

What are the odds that you go somewhere on vacation, meet someone most likely late thirties or early forties, attractive, in a relatively high profile job, and she has *never* been married?

Then again, a lot of guys, or maybe just guys my age, are often a bit slow to absorb the changes in the world. So what do I know?

Not wanting the reporter side of my brain to gallop off too far, too fast, I reached over and placed a hand on her forearm.

"Good for you," I said, letting my hand rest on her arm for a second and with her giving me a look of bemusement. I pulled it back and started cleaning up the remnants of the lunch.

"Why do you say 'good for me?"

I shrugged and leaned forward to fold the beach towel. Maybe I was getting a little too personal.

"Marriage is not for everyone. If you can avoid the heartache, maybe the expense and all the fighting over things when it doesn't work, and if you don't want a family and you aren't lonely, *why* get married? Even if you do want a family," I added, "a lot of people adopting kids these days."

Romey watched me gathering the napkins and the food containers. I took a drink of water and placed everything in the bag. She stood and brushed off the back of her slacks.

"Some of my married friends are very happy. And some," she rolled her eyes, "fight all the time."

"Must be something that only happens on this island."

She gave me the playful pat on the cheek, the same as she had the other night at The Tipsy when I was drinking the Goombay Smash. It was the very same evening that walking home, in silent conversation with myself, I'd had the suspicion that every third single guy who came through here – and maybe a few married ones – probably tried to put some moves on Romey McIntosh.

Twenty Five
Observation Deck

It was almost sunset and maybe thirty minutes to dusk when we pulled into the parking lot behind the vacation cottages back in Treasure Cay. Just two other cars in the lot, one of them shrouded in a custom-made blue car cover, likely owned by someone not planning to be around for a while.

"Can you come meet my friends?" I said. Romey looked at her watch. "I would like it if you could say hello."

"Yes, that would be nice," she said and opened her car door.

When we got to the cottage, Louie and Becky were not there and the door was locked. I knocked, took out my key, opened the door while saying, "Hello. I'm back." Never want to barge in on someone, eh? No response.

After checking their bedroom, I came back to the kitchen. Romey was still at the door.

"They probably went to the beach. Wanna' walk over there?"

"Okay."

Only a two-minute walk, the area of the beach closest

to the cottage had no people. All the chaise lounges had been pulled up above the tideline and were ready for tomorrow. I looked first to the left to see if I could spot them. Nope. Then way down at the far end, where we'd walked earlier in the week to see the impressive beachfront homes, I saw two people standing on a point near the water. Had to be Louie and Becky.

"I think that's them, down there," I said, pointing. I knew that it was maybe a thirty-minute walk if you weren't in a hurry.

Turning back to Romey, I gestured with my right arm to an observation deck that had been erected just above a dune behind us. It was there for folks who didn't want to deal with the sand. About the size of the deck on my house back in Vermont, it had four chaises and a couple deck chairs. It was painted in a color scheme close to matching the water, with white and pink accent on the railing and posts.

"Let's go there," I said. She followed me.

We arranged the deck chairs to face west, watched the sun drop out of sight and I became conscious that more than once today, we'd fall into these little non-talking, just gazing moments. Each time it happened, Romey had this lovely smile that was somewhere between bemusement and mischief. Then again, I'd pretty much thrown in the towel on trying to read a woman's thoughts.

I stood to see where Louie and Becky were now. It appeared they had moved about ten feet. Must have stayed down there to watch the sunset but now moving this way very slowly. Might be dark before they got here. I started to sit again but Romey got up from her chair as I turned around.

She glanced over her shoulder back toward the cottages behind us. There were a few seconds of silence before she said, "I must go soon. I can meet your friends tomorrow. You will bring them to Pizza Night?"

"Been waiting all week," I replied.

She placed her right hand on my left shoulder and gave me the smile. "Thank you for preparing the lunch today. I liked the cookies."

"Old family recipe," I said. "Thank you for all the driving. And the blue hole."

When she dropped her hand from my shoulder, she brushed my left hand and turned to go.

"Wait a second," I said. "I have another question."

She turned back to face me. We were maybe a foot apart. Now I placed my right hand on her shoulder. Come on, Hanlon.

"May I kiss you?" I said.

A slight tilt of the head, certainly bemusement in her eyes and the smile.

"Is that what you would like?" she said.

With my left hand, I touched her cheek and moved close in. She raised her head. The kiss was soft and lasted three days and fifteen minutes. I leaned back and looked at her. Then I gently put both arms around her. We kissed again. This time it was both of us.

"Well mudda sick," she said and laughed.

I walked with her to the car, no talking, holding hands like two ninth-graders after a movie. We kissed once again, she got in the car and managed to back around while also watching me. Then she was gone.

When I got back to the deck it was almost dark. The Ragsdales were coming off the beach, also holding hands.

Maybe it really was High School Hop night and Louie would put on a little DJ routine over dinner.

Twenty Six
Tomorrow

With the classroom work behind them, the RBPF officers in Cooper's Town would now have some physical activity outside the next morning. Nothing like the Police College days when they were young recruits, but a series of light drills. But first up was a short Q & A session and discussion of "what ifs" from all they had covered over the past three days.

Now seated at two tables, finishing their evening meal, the group was about to have an unannounced visitor: the Right Honorable Hubert Ingraham, former Prime Minister, highly regarded by many as a 'local hero' on Abaco.

Entering the room behind a resident member of the RBPF, Ingraham caught the surprised looks. He offered an informal salute and a warm smile. Everyone began to stand. With both hands pushing downward he motioned for them to be seated.

Dressed in a blue-checked shirt, no tie and a charcoal-colored suit darker than his short grey hair, Ingram looked like a slightly heavier, marginally shorter and twenty-years-younger brother of the actor Sidney Poitier, also a native Bahamian from Cat Island.

He walked around the tables, shaking hands with each officer, reading their name tags and welcoming them to Cooper's Town. When he came to Inspector Cynthia Knowles, he gave her a bear hug. Even though the Knowles family had known the PM since before she was born, she was still mildly embarrassed by this attention.

Ingraham went back to the front of the room and sat on the edge of a table. The RBPF officer who accompanied him stood off to one side.

"When I am at my office in Nassau, I have occasion to see Commissioner Greenslade," Ingraham said, referring to one Ellison Edroy Greenslade, the man at the head of the nation's police force and RBPF veteran of more than thirty-five years. He'd been appointed to that top post during Ingraham's last stint as Prime Minister.

"It is important for me to say, and I am sure that you know this already, that the Commissioner – and all of your fellow Bahamians – we are proud of your service and your dedication to our country." He placed his right hand just above his heart and added, "Thank you."

Ingraham shifted to get his rear end comfortable on the table, then continued.

"Since I was a little boy," he gestured to the windows with his right arm extended, "playing out there under my Granma's watchful eyes over sixty years ago, the world has changed more than my Granma could ever have imagined. And before you reach my age," he chuckled, "it will change more than *we* can possibly imagine." He paused to look at the group.

"Working together for a safer Bahamas is not just a slogan dreamed up by our administrative brothers and sisters on New Providence." Watching the officers as he went on, shifting from one face to the next, Ingraham's soft-spoken delivery was both measured and authoritative. The man had decades of experience in public speaking and was really good at it.

"It is not only the Commissioner that I have had the privilege of speaking with. Assistant Superintendent Harris was kind enough to pay me a visit this afternoon before going back to Nassau. She told me about the training this week.

One thing that she said about *all* of you," he waved his arm to include those seated and the officer who came in with him. He paused for a couple of seconds before continuing, again slowly shifting his gaze.

"Tomorrow, and every day in the future, what you do," he was now pointing with his right index finger, moving it around to underscore his words, "what *you* do will help to shape the future of our country." Dropping his arm, he clasped his hands together between his legs and leaned his shoulders backward.

"I say that, knowing very well as you also know, this will be true in the days to come, when more than a few of our fellow countrymen and some from away, will make the work dangerous. Every one of you possesses the courage, and the compassion, to lead your fellow officers and this outstanding force."

Sounding now more like a father, or a teacher offering encouragement for a challenging task, Ingraham stood, buttoned his jacket, then added, "That is why you are here today. You truly will be the stewards of our future."

He gave the informal salute again and turned to leave. The ten officers responded in spontaneous applause, which prompted Ingraham to turn quickly and smile, holding his right arm high above his head.

"Please, that is not necessary." The applause tapered off and the officers stood from their seats. "And, if I may add two brief comments," he said, arm still above his head.

"First, my visit has nothing to do with the election next spring." He was smiling broadly and the officers began to laugh. "Cooper's Town is very dear to me. Thank you for coming. And," he dropped his arm and pointed at them again, "I hope that you enjoy Pizza Night."

The smile went full wattage, he waved the arm high again and left the room.

Twenty Seven
Young Men

An objective observer could tell you that Joey was right at a tipping point. If and when the police in Marsh Harbour discovered his identity as the one who shot two Haitians, another view would be that Joey had already moved beyond that point.

Two brief encounters with Jameson, 'dat is my name, mon,' from Port-au-Prince and Joey was grasping for yet another way to try to leave Abaco. He now hoped that this was his ticket. Beyond clinging to this new, desperate belief that Jameson would actually help him, Joey worked hard to convince himself that there was also money to be made in the deal.

They had agreed to meet again, on Thursday night, just twenty-four hours away. Jameson claimed that he could get them on a boat and off the island. Joey needed to get his affairs in order and do whatever he needed to do before they left. Coming back to Marsh Harbour, for that matter *anywhere* on Abaco, was not in the cards, at least not in the foreseeable future.

Back in his apartment, Joey counted the cash he had

hidden in a white, one-gallon plastic jug on the bottom shelf in his refrigerator. He'd placed it behind a dish of food leftovers and two cans of beer. Inside the jug, wrinkled bills of mostly tens and twenties, a few fifties and hundreds, the total came to just shy of three thousand dollars. Not a lot when you're planning to leave, but he wasn't broke. And he was prepared to try anything once he was away from Abaco.

Do the dealing, do the running, do whatever it takes to make the transition to the 'Big Time', which in Joey's mind, held promise beyond the Bahamas. Maybe start on New Providence or Grand Bahama. But there were many other islands away from this chain and thousands of people *not* Bahamian.

His truck. A quick cash sale for less than it was really worth, a bargain for someone in The Mud. A small combo television and radio that he rarely used. Some of his clothes. Posters on the wall in his apartment. None of these things would leave with him.

One of the last things that Joey needed to do before leaving was to go see Atty. He would do that tomorrow. Late in the day would be better, before meeting Jameson.

Atty Gilbert possibly needed some form of medication. It was nothing that he thought about, but his sister considered it. In fact, part of her recent conversation with Romey had touched on the question.

"Has he ever been to the clinic or seen a doctor?" Romey had asked.

"Not since he was in school," Mirella had replied.

"That was years ago. But he is a healthy young man. You should see him." She held up a hand first to indicate that Atty was tall, then both hands to show broad.

The rest of that conversation had shifted to comments about how some people with emotional or psychological issues could sometimes benefit from certain medications. Unlike other places and cultures, Bahamians in general, were not given to pharmaceutical prescriptions, or so-called generic, over-the-counter drugs.

Many were familiar, however, with 'natural' remedies. While most people might not know the names of organic compounds such as tetrahydrocannabinol, THC, found in the resin secreted from the flowering plant Cannabis, they might know first-hand of the perceived benefits of toking up a little ganja.

Mirella had seen it much of her life, usually in younger men who gave the impression that not much would affect them and that they could float through anything that came their way. She had no knowledge, nor interest, in the claims of benefits derived from using marijuana. Reduce anxiety, reduce pain, soothe tremors, relieve joint aches, improve metabolism and produce all around 'feel good' effects? Not by Mirella's standards.

What she did know, and had a strong interest in, was her little brother. She would not allow him to get caught up in that life and be with those people, most notably Joey Aberle. After the talk with Romey and a lot of time to think during the drive to and from work, Mirella found a resolve that was about to come front and center on Atty's welfare.

Terrence would return late on Friday. Despite all of his tough talk and easy intimidation of Atty, she knew that her husband cared about the boy. With TD spending most of his time at his girlfriend's home and working, only visiting his parents on the weekend, Mirella saw how Atty could become useful.

Despite the way he acted, Terrence was not getting any younger. He was unlikely to admit it, but a little help with the maintenance of the boat and trailer, all the fishing gear, that could be one of the best steps they could take to help Atty to move beyond his frequent juvenile behavior. Maybe help him get centered, before he got into real trouble.

Twenty Eight
Gotta Be Mutual

Often there are times when it is impossible to read the cause, or random thought, that triggers Louie Ragsdale's smirk. Sometimes it morphs from a look of derision into one of playful good humor, like we're sharing a joke that nobody else will get.

All evening, ignoring his wife's repeated exclamations, "Louie! Stop that." Or, "Enough, already." And my favorite, "Do you want to go to your room?" None of these seemed to drain one ounce from Louie's pleasure in giving me the razz.

I never found the ribbing to be mean-spirited or the form of put-down humor that gets old really fast. Usually there was this unspoken plea in the wisecracks, begging for more common sense from the person on the receiving end. Yet he was not above the fairly normal 'guy stuff'. And that's what much of the past two hours had been. Pour it on.

Watching him across the living room, bare feet on the coffee table, flipping through a magazine and taking sips of beer, each time he glanced up he gave me the 'you know that I know' look. And I guess that I *did* know that he knew. If Becky knew, she used a woman's good judgement to just let it roll. No need to snoop.

It started after Romey had left earlier and I'd waited at the Observation Deck for the Ragsdales to come from the beach. The three of us walking back to the cottage and me babbling on about my day: the blue hole, the group of police officers in Cooper's Town and Romey's cousin, having lunch along the water, looking out a Green Turtle Cay, watching the sunset and waiting so they could meet her.

The last tidbit caused Louie to stop mid-step, turn to me and take hold of both my shoulders. Becky had taken a couple of steps before she turned to hear her husband coming after me.

"Hanlon. Please tell me. Not again." And even though it would be another few minutes before Becky caught on, I knew immediately that Ragsdale was aiming for what he thought was my fickleness with women.

While I was cooking chicken breasts on the grill, Louie came to the patio with two bottles of beer, doing his low volume singing, "*Chuck E's in love. What could make a boy behave this way?*"

I shook my head and got up from the chair. That only egged him on. He scooted over and placed his arms around Becky and began making little kisses next to her ear before she pushed him away. He laughed and held his bottle up in a toast.

Our friendship had evolved to a point where Louie, too

easily, could and would hone in on my quirks. Each time I became aware of this, the self-defense mechanisms kicked in. I would try to find ways to deflect the attention or redirect the conversation. He never fell for it. Maybe back off a little, just for a few minutes, but then he was ready to nudge it again at the next opportunity.

Eventually Becky and Louie went to bed. I sat up reading. One of the books in my friend Bill's collection was an old copy of Hunter S. Thompson's *Gonzo Papers Vol. I – The Great Shark Hunt*, an amusing collection of essays and some pretty outrageous stuff. A lot of it made me laugh out loud. The quotes in the book from one Raoul Duke provided a little insight for understanding some of the *Doonesbury* comic strip re-runs in our daily paper back home.

By the time I was ready for bed, I was thinking about relationships, good and bad, how men approach them and react, and how that is just so, so different from the way most women handle things. Considering Louie and Becky reminded me of something my older sister Laura said years ago about the couples who stay together for a long time.

"Respect. No matter the ups and downs, the good times and the really shitty periods. We all have heartaches at one time or another. The *friendship* is important," she'd said, adding "Love when you can keep it, and whatever it means to you." I could still see her face when she was giving me her little dissertation on domestic tranquility.

"When a couple can keep mutual respect for one another, that's gonna' go a long way in how they cope with everything else." I remembered thinking at the time that she and her husband must've had few difficult innings.

Then again, I never quizzed my sister, or anyone else, regarding 'people chemistry'. When two people meet, what is the first trigger that begins the process of attraction? Pheromones? Eyes? A smile? Body size and shapes? A person's laugh? Empathy?

I turned the ceiling fan up a notch and switched off the bedside lamp before falling asleep. My last stream of marginally connected thoughts skimmed over the question of how one's feelings might be influenced by Goombay Smash and being on vacation.

Twenty Nine
Romey

Nearly half of her life working for the same employer. That was good. Romey was raised to believe in working hard and being responsible, virtues that went hand-in-hand. For those who adhered to this ethic, it became as much a part of who you *are* as any personality trait.

Caring for others was instilled early with the McIntosh children. As the second born with two brothers and three sisters, Romey had had a chance to put this into practice early in childhood when she was called on to help her mother with the younger siblings. She had enjoyed the role, never thinking of it as some infringement on her own life, then or now.

Boys. They were the puzzle to Romey as an adolescent. She certainly *liked* boys, enjoyed all manner of childhood games, much of this with church related activities when she was younger. But just about the time she turned thirteen, things changed. The attention she received from the boys was different than it had been. And older boys began teasing her as well.

Her mama had had many things to say about this and for several years, all the way through high school, the reassurance and explanations from mama had made the difference. By the time she was eighteen, Romey's poise and self-confidence had become more obvious.

The winter following her graduation from high school, Romey had gotten her first real job at the resort. She started as a waitress in the main restaurant and did that for nearly ten years before she was asked to sub for a bartender who was ill. It was during a busy week when one of the fishing tournaments had come to Treasure Cay.

With a lot of guidance from an older, seasoned bar tender, coupled with her easy-going personality and hard work, Romey had been a hit. The older bartender, also a woman, had told the resort manager that Romey was a 'natural'.

Through all the years since the short-lived romance when she was only twenty, Romey had avoided chances to have a boyfriend or intimate relationships. She could and did flirt and had fun, but resisted serious involvement with a man. That was not an easy thing to do.

Occasionally, Romey and some of the other women who worked at the resort would laugh about and imitate the men who tried to coax them into an affair. The women who worked at the *bar* or as *waitresses* learned soon enough that dealing with suggestive comments and come-ons from men, often drunk, was a part of the job. The younger, more attractive women got the brunt of the overtures.

Only a few weeks into her new job as a bartender, after an incident when one man – a tourist from the US – had become difficult to discourage, Romey had gotten sound advice from her boss.

"First time they say something makes you uncomfortable, stop them. 'I do not want to hear that talk, thank you.' That's what you tell them." The woman who had told her this watched Romey to be sure that it sank in, then repeated it. "I do not want to hear that talk. Then you tell *me* who is this be talking that way."

Now, coming up on ten years behind the bar, thousands and thousands of customers later, Romey had developed the skills and the attitude that made her the most popular employee at the resort. A side benefit was that she got lots of generous tips.

The biggest day of the week, Thursday, was one she always looked forward to, Pizza Night. Romey, two other women and one man, would mix and serve more than a thousand drinks before the evening was over. Preparing for work today was like any other day. Except for one minor blip. Her mind was wandering just a bit as she got ready to go to work.

Much of the previous evening, beginning with the drive home from TC on her day off, had been spent circling around thoughts and questions about what had just happened. And replaying those thoughts and questions, Romey had become aware of a clearly perceptible jolt to her senses.

Now, driving down the SC Bootle highway, a trip she could make blind-folded, Romey spent more time than usual noticing the trees, the birds, the sky, people riding bicycles, all the things she saw every day. The difference was that all of these everyday sightings seemed to have more clarity, a sharper focus, in contrast with her thoughts and questions.

Who is this Michael Hanlon was the main question? She remembered a golf pro who worked at the resort a few years ago and who had spent many evenings at the bar. He was always pointing out Americans and would tell Romey that they were probably CIA. It was not an uncommon perception among resort employees. She didn't believe it and didn't think that about this man from Vermont.

When she'd stepped from the shower earlier this morning, Romey had found a week-old newspaper that showed an election map of the US and found Vermont way up in the corner, close to Canada. It was tiny, not much bigger than some of the islands. How many people could live in such a small place?

Slowing for the speed bump ahead and the security booth entering the village of Treasure Cay, she knew that she could come up with an entire list of questions for Michael Hanlon. Information about a very small province and its small population would be at the bottom of the list.

Romey parked the car, turned off the engine and sat

for a minute. The men trimming the shrubbery along the entrance to the resort pushed a cart in front of her and moved on to the next building. Two young housekeeping women, wearing the company uniform of tan slacks with floral print shirts, walked by her carrying towels and toiletries for the guest rooms. Romey watched the women, recalling when she was their age and began working here.

'May I kiss you?' Well, we will see about you, Mr. Hanlon.

Thirty
Da Mud

On any given day brief periods of chaos might be the scene around the criss-crossing, narrow paths that run through The Mud. Imagine older, busy streets and alleys found in some rundown urban neighborhood with too many people on the move all at the same time. Only here in The Mud, the 'buildings' weren't rundown, they could barely stand in the first place.

And only chaotic if you were an outsider. To the hundreds of people who lived there, it was the way things are. Barefoot children, a few dogs, some goats, chickens, any number of adults, all out going somewhere within the community. Watch your step, especially after a heavy rain, not to mention Category 4 hurricanes.

The family who had allowed Jameson to stay in their already overcrowded house was actually a young nephew from Haiti, his wife and two children. Now, after three days on Abaco, Jameson told his nephew that he would be leaving tonight. This came as no surprise. Jameson had appeared with little notice and had spent most of his time with two other older Haitian men who lived in The Mud.

There had been no shared meals or any 'family time' at the nephew's house.

After returning very late the previous night, it was now early afternoon when Jameson awoke, got dressed and again went off somewhere. It was not clear if he was coming back before his planned departure. The nephew didn't know and didn't ask.

Back at the blue house, where a few men often gathered, Jameson met with two fellow-countrymen. He'd known of them back in Haiti and they had now been on Abaco for several months. They would be considered illegal migrants as neither had a work permit to be there.

Deportation was not a concern to Jameson. His plan all along had been to find out what happened when two previously assigned 'runners' had been shot, probably robbed, and to then determine the likelihood of future activity out of Marsh Harbour. He had the information that he needed on both questions and now it was time to leave.

While many residents of The Mud, especially the men, might have had suspicions about the activities of Jameson and his ilk, any questions were always asked carefully and nobody was going to say anything. It was extremely unlikely that *anyone* would say a word to the police. All of the adults who lived in The Mud knew that, short of extreme violence, brutality or murder, nobody was going to do or say something that could bring a visit from the RBPF.

"Be da same place we land before. We see light on da

boat, da raft leaves da beach," the man said to Jameson. With two fingers of his right hand, he pointed and added, "Jus' you and me."

Jameson nodded, reached into his pants pocket and pulled out a crushed pack of cigarettes. He offered the pack to the man across from him. The man took one. Jameson handed him his lighter, waited, then lighted his own cigarette. He took a deep drag, tilted his head back and blew smoke into the air. He looked at the man that he knew only as Clancy.

"We leave from here?" Jameson asked. The man removed the cigarette from his lips and moved his head slowly in the affirmative.

"Das' it. Go to da docks, walk up da beach. Den wait." Clancy took another hit on the cigarette. "I come back wit da raft. When we see da signal, is only five minutes from da beach."

There was no discussion about anyone else to be accompanying Jameson. If that were to happen, it could be dealt with when it was time.

Thirty One
Food

Standing just a foot from Cynthia Knowles, Inspector Denny Ring pointed at the two youngest officers in the training session, Team Coconut. One was an officer from Andros and the other was from Bimini.

"Let them go have pizza," Ring said. He looked at Knowles and nodded his head in a quick, exaggerated manner. "We can get conch fritters, peas and rice, some boiled crabs. Have some Kalick. Dinner right here," he added, pointing out to the water.

Knowles looked at him as though he was suggesting that they climb aboard a UFO at the TC Airport. She tilted her head forward, chin nearly touching her clavicle, scrunched her face into a half-smile and moved her eyes back and forth rapidly.

"That is a grand idea," she said. "It's just what we will do. Maybe two cases of beer." She looked around the lawn area surrounding the building where they'd been inside for three days. Now she pointed in the direction of the water just a stone's throw away.

"And you be the one call the Commissioner, yes? Tell

him we be having a party, is that OK?" she said. Ring didn't answer.

"Ask him if it is also OK that we have some music. Perhaps get a DJ." Ring turned to walk away from her. He was shaking his head, bobbing his shoulders like a boxer trying to loosen up. Knowles laughed at him.

"You want me to get his phone number for you?" she said. Ring kept walking.

"Inspector Ring," she called. He stopped and turned back to face her.

"We *all* be going to Pizza Night." She looked at her watch. "At 5 o'clock," she added. Ring turned mumbling to himself.

"Perhaps you call your friend the Honourable Hubert Ingraham." He was careful not to utter this loud enough for Knowles to actually hear what he said.

Each island in the Bahamas has dishes that are favored by the inhabitants. Throughout the country, some of the most popular dishes include stewed conch with dough boys, or dumplings; pigeon peas and rice; tropical fruits; pork; grouper chowder and various dishes and salads that include shell fish.

As in many lightly populated places in the developed world, sometime around two or three generations back, pizza showed up. First in pizza/sub shops. Then boxed mixes with ingredients for dough, sauce and cheese, all available in food stores. Later on, menus in all types of restaurants routinely included pizza. Today, frozen and fresh, ready-to-bake varieties with different types of dough are widely available. And they can be ready in a matter of minutes right there in your kitchen.

It is uncertain when pizza arrived here, or on which island, most likely New Providence, possibly Bimini. Not much different from other places, people liked it and pizza caught on.

The first Pizza Night at The Tipsy Seagull went back more than twenty-five years. It was part of an experiment with various 'theme' nights at the resort. Initially, it wasn't held every week. The toppings offered for the pizzas were pretty basic, nothing really creative. The change most likely occurred during one of the popular, week long fishing tournaments that moved around each year to different islands.

When the small marina at Treasure Cay is full of boats and the resort and condos have peak occupancy, there can be a real mix of people coming for dinner, many from the US. Then there are the locals and the folks coming in by boat from other nearby islands.

With the addition of live music a few years ago, now featuring Chris 'Da' Burner, it has become a big deal. Newspaper ads and posters refer to the evening as Abaco's 'Largest Social Event.' Excluding the annual winter Junkanoo celebrations and heritage festivals held on the different islands, the claim is not that big of a stretch.

The busiest Pizza Night of the year will see nearly six-hundred pizzas made in just over five hours. Most of those are consumed on the premises. It might be interesting to get some comparable data on the busiest pizza shops in say, New York City, Chicago, Boston or Los Angeles.

An enterprising free-lance writer for *Abaco Life* once did a little research on pizza consumption. Susie Wright, an Indiana college student at the time who frequently visited the island with family, composed what became a feature article. She found, among other things, that in the US there are more than 60,000 pizzerias; the average person eats nearly fifty slices a year; approximately four million pizzas are sold the day of the Super Bowl and more than *five billion* pizzas are sold world-wide every year.

Wright was unable to find meaningful pizza statistics pertaining specifically to the Bahamas. She did say that her favorite toppings included artichoke hearts, black olives, caramelized onions and feta cheese, and that she preferred thin crispy crust rather than thick crust.

Thirty Two
Women

Becky Ragsdale went back to the cottage to shower. Louie and I stayed at the beach. The plan was that we would come up in a few minutes, clean up, then all of us would head for The Tipsy early enough to get a table near the marina.

"So, you wanna' tell me about her?" Louie said as soon as Becky was out of earshot. Closing my book, placing my right index finger between the pages to mark my spot, I looked at him.

Reaching down under the chaise I pulled my wrist watch out of my sandals. I already knew the time. Becky had just told us that it was 4:15 before she went to the cottage. Making a point of studying the face of the watch, I looked back at him.

"Has your wife ever timed how long you can go without that self-satisfied expression?" The reply was a barely audible chuckle, a pursing of his lips like he might whistle and a gesture with both hands like he'd just tossed something into the air.

"So?" he repeated.

"So? Tell you about *whom*?" Now he laughed out loud, sat up and turned around sideways on his chaise. He placed both feet in the sand and pulled his sunglasses down to the tip of his nose.

"Don't go all proper there, Radio Rick. I've watched you for a while now," he said. "You get around some '*lovely*' as you call them, and your eyes start to cross. You walk funny. And your chatter goes from 45 rpm to 78! Kinda' nervous like, know what I mean?" Another chuckle.

But he held his cocky posture, sitting just two feet away and determined that he would provoke some response. I found my bookmark, slipped it between the pages and placed the book on my lap.

"I prefer to think that my *stamina* makes me more like an LP. You remember them, 33 rpm? And, should I recline here before we go on? Maybe you can take notes."

"Whatever works for you, partner," he said.

Instead, I sat up and adjusted the backrest to an upright position. I took a deep, cleansing breath, held it, then blew out through my mouth.

"Where to begin? You see, when I was about ten, there was this amazingly beautiful teenage girl in my town. She was maybe fifteen or sixteen. I think later she became an actress."

"Go ahead, wise guy. Try to duck it," Louie said. He laughed again, then added, "You are finally showing signs of recovery from the divorce. What, three years ago?"

"Almost four," I said.

"A few months ago, the very young and," he held his fingers up to make air quotation marks, "lovely" Bonnie, said sayonara, I'm outa' here." He waited for me to respond. Nope.

"Then you hit fifty and, later than most it would seem, jump on the mid-life crisis bus. Bullshit!"

Just listening I could tell that Louie was approaching take-off. I knew the pattern. One of his 'I'm just trying to help out here' routines. When he starts, one doesn't find many opportunities to say, 'but wait'. He just keeps moving through the lecture.

Now he moved to the edge of the chaise and took off his sunglasses. The smirk was gone, he looked a tad more serious.

"Did you ever watch *Northern Exposure* back in the day?" he said.

"Yeah. Great writing. I really liked the Ed character."

"So you also remember the radio guy? Chris in the Morning."

"Of course. He's done a lot of movies since then, right?"

"Maybe. But, in one of the episodes he's doing his morning bit on air, and he does a little monologue about women. Talking about all shapes, sizes, their hair, their smile, their eyes. *What is it* that first attracts us to them?" Louie paused to be sure that I was listening. "I think the camera showed all of the different women from the show as he went through his spiel," Louie added.

"Yeah, I did see that episode. Wasn't he all hot for the woman pilot?"

"Nah, that was the doc. From New York." He let that hang there, waiting for me to speak. I continued to wait him out. Now he went mute. Finally, I turned around and placed my feet on the sand, facing him.

"So, your point *is*?" I said.

"Christ, Hanlon. DO YOU WANT TO TELL ME ABOUT HER?" he said, slowly enunciating each word. "Your," again the air quotation marks, "lovely" Romea, Romey for short. The one who has you wading out there just a little deeper into goofy."

"Goofy?"

"OK, never mind," he said, reaching down to pull on his flip-flops. "Tell Becky if you like. She'll set you straight. But don't bullshit her, though. She'll pick up on that before you can say bonefish at one o'clock."

"We'll meet her when we go over to The Tipsy. You and Becky give me your reaction. Don't want to prejudice anybody, eh?"

"Can't wait," was Louie's wiseass reply.

Terrence Williams called his wife when he came in from guiding. He would be staying on Eluthera for another night and planned to take his two sports out again the next morning, then they would head back to Marsh Harbour.

Mirella told her husband about the plan to take Atty up to Treasure Cay for Pizza Night. He thought it was a good idea. They talked about TD and his home-away-from home at the girlfriend's. She did not mention to Terrence anything about her other idea, for Atty to help him with boat maintenance and chores related to the guide service. That discussion could wait.

"I love you, Terrence. You be careful, hear?" she said.

"Always careful. You know 'dat. I love you."

"Bye, baby" she said, clicked off the phone and placed it on the bathroom vanity.

When she came out of the bathroom, Atty was outside on the deck off the kitchen. He was doing something with his phone, not talking. Texting. Mirella stood at the door and watched him for a minute before speaking.

"Atty. We're going to leave at 5:30," she said. Still fixated on the phone, he nodded but didn't respond. She was about to ask him whom he was texting, changed her mind, turned to the bedroom to get into different clothes.

Mirella realized after her conversation with Terrence that she didn't worry so much anymore about her own son. Compared to Atty, TD seemed years older, more mature and was clearly crazy about his girlfriend, which probably helped to keep him in line. If she had any real concern about her son it was that he would get his girlfriend pregnant before they were married, or at least committed to staying together as a couple.

She knew that whatever happened, they would make

it work. If a baby came along, it would not be the first time in her family that one arrived before a nine-month anniversary of the wedding day. Removing her slacks, she folded them and placed them over a chair, then pulled on a skirt that she'd selected earlier. Thoughts about the possibility of a baby triggered other thoughts. As she pulled her hair back and twisted a band around it, she looked in the mirror and tried to imagine how she would be as a grandmother. That made her smile.

Mirella knew that she would be a good Nonnie, just like her mother's mother, who loved every one of her twenty-six grandchildren. She laughed at the memory of her own mother-in-law, Terrence's mother, who early on had informed her offspring that she was too glamorous to be a grandmother. She said that all of *their* children should call her Glamma.

Reaching into the bottom of the closet Mirella pulled out a pair of sandals and sat on the edge of the bed. She slipped the shoes on, stood, and with both hands brushed the front of her shirt to smooth it over her breasts and stomach. She repeated the motion, then stopped abruptly and turned her head to the door.

There were voices in the living room. The television? She listened. No, she could hear Atty's voice. He wouldn't talk to the television. He didn't even like watching it.

Mirella smoothed her shirt again and went to the bedroom door.

Thirty Three
Right Now

"Ou konprann?" the man had said. Joey nodded. Now he was tempted to use the Creole expression on Atty, but he wouldn't get it; 'Do you understand?'

Just an hour earlier, Joey had watched Jameson's back when he turned away from him following a tense exchange about how Joey would dispose of his truck. The man from Port 'au Prince had made it clear that *that* was not his problem. He strongly suggested that the best thing Joey could do was to make a deal with some Haitian, possibly his nephew, and not worry about coming up short on the price.

Then before declaring the 'konprann' ultimatum, the man had listened as Joey described how he needed to settle things with a friend before leaving Abaco. It had become clear that the dynamic of this new relationship with Jameson had shifted. No longer was he asking questions and showing curiosity about Joey's contacts on the island.

The man had taken on the demeanor of someone giving orders and expecting immediate compliance.

"It would not be well for you to," he had paused, "hesitate, mon," Jameson had said. His cold stare conveyed more than the words. But just in case Joey misunderstood, the man had stepped closer to him and almost whispered, "You should do this. Right now, mon." Then delivered the emphatic, "Ou konprann?"

As soon as Jameson was out of sight, Joey had gone off to find Atty. The text messages back and forth confirmed that Atty was at his sister's home, a few minutes away. Joey had asked if Terrence was there. Atty texted back, 'Not here. Fishing.'

And now Joey was there at the house with Atty.

It was dark, scattered lights coming on around The Mud. Jameson threw his long legs over one of the bar stools inside the blue house, the informal gathering spot used by a small group of Haitians out of hundreds living here.

Across the room sat three other men and one woman, none of whom were known to him. Jameson only knew the owner of the house, who was sitting directly opposite him.

"Clancy say that you be goin," the man said. "Tonight?" He poured two glasses of dark rum, placed one in front of Jameson and took a sip from the other.

Jameson nodded. He glanced at the others before speaking.

"I have nothing else here on Abaco." He pronounced it a-*Boke*-o. "Friends in Nassau are waiting."

159

"You will come back, another time?" the man said. Jameson studied the man's face.

"It will depend," he answered, again looking at the three men and the woman seated in the corner of the room. All of them held drinks and seemed to be in a gay mood, talking and laughing, mostly in Haitian Creole mixed with some English, not showing interest in Jameson.

He turned back to the man. They'd never met before Jameson had arrived three days earlier. Now he was intrigued.

"You know this Joey? Lives in Marsh Harbour," Jameson said.

"The tall one," the man replied. He looked at Jameson. "Like you," he added. Jameson nodded.

"Was here before. Another man brought him. We had the ladies one evening. Music and dancing."

"He is a Bahamian. Does he have a job?" Jameson asked. The man shrugged.

"I do not know this." He held his right hand up and rubbed his thumb and two fingers together to indicate money. "Lajan kach," he added. "When he was here the other time. Paying for all the drinks."

Jameson thought about that before asking the next question. "Did you know the boys who were shot? Police found them with a boat." The man shook his head.

"Stupid. I never see them here." He shook his head again. "They were taken from the hospital, to Nassau I heard." As he said this, the man looked at Jameson.

"Maybe your friends in Nassau know more. Moun sot," he tacked on for good measure.

Jameson agreed the two might be 'idiots'. Or just jacked up on what they skimmed from the product they were attempting to sell.

Standing to his full six-foot-three, Jameson pulled a Bahamian ten-dollar bill from his pocket and placed it on the counter in front of the man.

"Mesi," he said, thanking the man for the glass of rum. He walked out into the night.

One last visit to say goodbye to the nephew. Leave him some money. Then Jameson would make the decision about this Joey.

Thirty Four
Beat The Crowd

Two RBPF vehicles were heading south on the SC Bootle Highway. The white Jeep Wrangler was in front driven by Constable Roos. The passengers were Inspectors Cythina Knowles and Denny Ring, along with two other officers, Hamilton and Walker, also part of the training group.

The powder blue Ford van that followed was one of only two police vans on the entire island. In addition to the driver, it carried five more RBPF officers. The two drivers kept a safe distance between vehicles travelling at a steady fifty-five miles per hour. It was unknown if they were using cruise control.

Slowing to make the turn in the direction of Treasure Cay, three customers and a checkout clerk inside a corner convenience store watched the police vehicles go by. No lights, no apparent urgency. Still, unusual for early on a quiet Thursday evening.

Rolling to almost a full stop at the small security hut located at the entrance to TC, the woman behind the glass inside the hut looked up as the Jeep approached. Knowles, the front seat passenger on the left, gave the woman an abbreviated salute with her left hand. The woman waved in response. The Ford van came next. Front seat passenger waved and got a wave in return.

As the two vehicles passed the security hut and a traffic control speed-breaker bump in the road, it took all of five seconds for the woman behind the glass to figure it out; these people were going to Pizza Night.

We walked along the sidewalk between the cottages and Becky stopped to smell blossoms on one of the bushes.

"What are those?" I asked.

"Flowers," Louie said. Such a clever guy. Becky stepped away from one bush, bent forward and sniffed another.

"The light pink is oleander," she said. "These," she leaned in a bit closer to a darker, almost violet flower, "are bougainvillea. They really don't have a scent." She sniffed again. I sniffed the lighter pink blossoms.

"Not a whole lot going on with this one, either," I said. Louie rolled his eyes.

"They're both very pretty. And someone here pays attention to pruning. But no real fragrance," Becky added.

"What's that great smell from the flowers down at the beach?" I asked.

"There's some Angel's Trumpet over by the wall. I can smell coconut flowers. And frangipani," she replied.

"Hanlon wouldn't know frangipani from scallopini," Louie yukked.

"And, naturally, you would." I said. "I seriously doubt it." We kept walking.

"Thin slices of meat. Maybe chicken, or veal. A little tomato wine sauce," Louie offered.

Crossing the street, the path along the parking lot behind The Tipsy must have had a dozen or more golf carts lined up, as well as a few bicycles. I looked at my watch; almost ten of six. We could hear voices and music coming from the direction near the pool and marina, just the on other side of the building. That's where we were headed.

Romey McIntosh had three others working with her at the bar tonight. Customers were beginning to arrive, mostly families, some with younger children. It was early and the drink orders, at least those for beer, wine and mixed beverages, wouldn't pick up until later.

Standing near the long buffet table where orders were placed for pizzas, Romey talked with one of the waitresses. By the time the crowd peaked, normally around 7:30 or 8, seven waitresses would be moving quickly back and forth among the tables bringing out trays of pizza and other food.

Each customer placing an order would take a stainless steel rod on a base, about eighteen inches high and holding a numbered card, and would then place it in the center of his table. The numbered cards were large enough for waitresses to see while moving through the crowd.

Romey watched Michael Hanlon and his two friends coming up the walk. She stepped out and waved. Michael saw her, smiled and raised his arm. She turned to look around at the restaurant area, spotted a table near the boardwalk and gestured in that direction. He waved again and started in that direction. By the time the three had arrived at the table, Romey was standing next to one of the chairs.

"Good evening," Romey said. Michael was quick to pick up on the smile that had gotten his attention a few nights earlier, the night of the Goombay Smash when the two of them flirted at the bar. Taking her left hand, he pulled it up and gave it a light kiss.

"Good evening," he said. She was mildly surprised and maybe a little embarrassed. She looked around to see if anyone had witnessed the gesture. Michael turned to his friends.

"Becky, this is Romey McIntosh," he said. The two women smiled and shook hands.

"Very nice to meet you," Becky said.

"And this is Becky's husband, Louie," Michael added. Ragsdale shook hands with Romey.

"Hello."

"You should take this table," Romey said, releasing Louie's hand. She turned to look out at the marina, then added, "As soon as people start coming from the boats, it will get busy."

Among the vessels tied up in the marina, a number of boats had people who were enjoying cocktails and laughing. Hanlon looked out at the boats. A few were larger than the others, and each with an impressive array of expensive electronic gear mounted on the bridge. He turned to Ragsdale and pointed at the boats.

"More friends of Dick Cheney," he said.

"I'm sure," was Louie's comeback.

"Let me get you something to drink," Romey said. "When you are ready, you can go over and place an order for pizza."

Thirty Five
Canine Ranking

Mirella came into the living room and couldn't believe her eyes. Standing at the front door was that no good Joey Aberle, talking with Atty. Her disbelief was quickly overtaken by the anger she felt that he would dare to come to her house.

"What are *you* doing here," she yelled, starting toward him. Joey stepped back from the door. He looked at Atty, then back to Mirella.

"I would like to talk with your brother," he said, casually pointing at Atty.

Mirella threw both arms in the air as if she were shooing away a flock of birds. She took another step closer to the door and repeated the motion with her arms.

"You be gone from here. Now," she yelled. "You having nothing to do with Atty." Joey didn't move. The woman was clearly crazy. He was not leaving until he had a word with Atty.

Joey had known one of two things would happen. He could trust that Atty would be quiet about past activities, in some of which he had participated, others when he had merely been an observer. If he could make himself really believe that Atty would not talk, then he would give him some money, maybe even the truck.

The other possibility was that trusting Atty was not such a good plan. If that turned out to be where Joey's thinking went, the outcome would be much less considerate.

Now this crazy woman was standing directly in front of Joey, nearly a foot shorter, eyes filled with rage, both hands folded into fists and held on her hips.

"Everyone in Marsh Harbour know about you, Joey Aberle," she said. Now raising her right hand, pointing a finger close to his face, she held his stare.

"You never work. You smoke dat dope. You probably a drunk. And you *no good* to your family. I remember all of dis," she said.

Now moving away from him, she stood in front of her brother to shield him from Joey and added one further observation.

"Dog betta dan you."

Bahamian women and men are similar to other ethnic groups. When conversing, arguing or pleading, it can begin to sound slightly different from a normal discussion. It's not unusual for people of a particular culture, especially when talking among themselves, to drift into a vocabulary and cadence that may be confusing to an outsider.

Specific words and expressions, sometimes coupled with a dose of profanity and stated through dramatic inflection or charged emotion, can serve to underscore the meaning of the actual utterance. From childhood on, such phrases quickly convey both what the speaker is thinking and *feeling*. If you happen to be on the receiving end, there is rarely any doubt. 'Dog betta dan you' is one such phrase.

In this particular instance, in this doorway in front of this woman, Joey Aberle not only had no doubt, he knew that his decision had to be quick.

One of the text message responses that Joey had received earlier from Atty had said that Terrence Williams was away and would not be returning tonight. It was for this reason that Joey had decided that he could show up without the added fear of being confronted by the big man. Joey was taller than most men. Terrence was both tall *and* big. He probably outweighed Joey by fifty pounds and none of it was fat.

But this little woman was no match. Joey could handle her. It was unpredictable how Atty might behave. Joey decided to play it safe and make it quick.

Pulling the .38 from the pocket of his jacket, Joey held it up so both Atty and his crazy sister could see the gun. Then he stepped into the room and closed the door behind him.

Thirty Six
Get In Line

Romey went behind the bar, mixed two Goombay Smashes and took a bottle of Kalick from the cooler. She placed them on a tray and returned to Michael Hanlon and his friends.

"You can't join us, I guess," Hanlon said as she placed the drinks on the table in front of them. She shook her head.

"I will have to start working soon." She motioned to the others behind the bar and added, "It will take all of us to keep up when the music starts." She laughed, then said, "I will come back to check on you."

"That would be really nice," Hanlon said.

"*Real-ly*?" Romey said, turning away.

As soon as she had left the table and gone back to the area where customers were now forming a line to order their pizzas, Louie reached over and took Hanlon's left hand. He pretended to kiss it before Hanlon pulled the hand away. Ragsdale laughed.

"Say, Lover Boy." He squeezed Hanlon's left bicep, then added, "Aren't *you* just the charmer?"

"You're impossible," Becky said to her husband, then to Hanlon, "Louie's idea of being romantic is to bring me coffee in the morning."

Hanlon reached over and raised Becky's left hand and gave it a light kiss. He raised his drink to toast her, then held his plastic drink cup for Louie join the toast with his beer.

The RBPF Constable walked at the front of the group approaching the outside dining area at The Tipsy Seagull. Roos was the only person in uniform; navy pants with a wide red stripe down the legs, light blue short-sleeve shirt and navy policeman's hat with a red band around it and a gold emblem at its center.

Those seated near the entrance noticed Roos, but not everyone connected him to the ten who followed. The group stopped and took in the crowd. Inspector Knowles knew the layout of the dining area. She saw a couple of vacant tables near the pool with chairs turned inward against the tables. Knowles stepped forward and motioned for her colleagues move in that direction.

As they went across the dining area, Romey spotted them. She made her way to the tables and arrived just behind the group. Everyone was moving around, arranging the chairs to take a seat. Cynthia Knowles had her back to Romey.

"I am so sorry. These tables are reserved," Romey said. A couple of the men started to get up from the chairs. Knowles turned and both women laughed.

"That is all right. We have a VIP connection with your manager's office," Cyndy said.

Some of the men now recognized Romey as the woman they'd seen when the car had stopped in Cooper's Town, when she had gotten out to speak with Knowles.

"Please. We are just foolin," Romey said. She motioned for everyone to be seated.

"I will come back to take your drink orders. If you are hungry, someone should get in line soon to order pizza."

I watched Romey walk across the room to chat with her cousin. Looking at them in profile, even at a distance of thirty feet or so, I could see a resemblance that was not apparent yesterday when we stopped the car and Romey had gotten out. Same nose, same lovely complexion, a couple of inches difference in height. The cousin was taller.

When I turned to Louie, he was watching, too. Becky was distracted by a couple of energetic kids and their mother trying to control them at the table next to us.

"I think they're cops," I said, without disclosing any of my previously obtained information.

Louie looked directly at me calling up a mock surprise expression. "Mister Private Eye. You are just *so* fast," he responded.

"The woman is Romey's cousin. RBPF," I said.

Louie took a drink of his beer, put the bottle on the table and leaned closer. He crooked a finger and motioned for me to lean in.

"I would imagine that all of them are RBPF, don't you think?" he said in an exaggerated whisper.

"The guy in the uniform. He might be a decoy." Becky turned when she heard me say this. It took her a second to see where we were looking. She spotted the uniformed officer seated with the others, turned to look at Louie and then at me.

"You don't think that man's a real policeman?" she said.

"I'm sure he's real. Your husband is just playing his little game," I said. Turning to Ragsdale I added, "Louie. Why don't you go say hello? Becky and I can get the pizza."

"No anchovies," he said. Becky stared at her husband for a beat.

"You're not going to go over there," she said. He shook his head.

"I'm not going anywhere."

Activity was picking up. By the time we got to place our order, I made a calculation of the crowd to be more than two-hundred. Behind us, probably another twenty-five people in line.

We'd studied the multi-colored menu that listed all the of the toppings for the pizza, no fewer than twenty combinations. I noticed that at the very top of the sheet it read *Pizza Pizazz*. From the hype Romey had given me when she had first told me about this event, I had concluded that you could come up with a custom mix of toppings and that the staff working away back there would make it for you.

Becky said that she would only eat one slice, but that she wanted to order a salad, too. So, we agreed on an extra-large pizza, ten slices. I asked for black olives, onions, tomatoes and mushrooms. And could they put some fresh conch meet on half of the pizza? Yes, they could. We paid for the order and the young man gave us a skinny metal rod on a stand to take back to the table. It was number 87.

Music was playing when we arrived. First, it was coming from a guy with a keyboard and some digital mixer device up near the bar. Now a man came out wearing a white Panama hat, dark blazer over a white silk shirt, open at the collar, with matching silk handkerchief folded in the front pocket. He had on bright green slacks, matching socks and white patent leather shoes.

The man carried a wireless mic, had a big smile and waved to the audience. Many in the crowd seemed to know him and they gave a round of applause with a few hoots and some whistling.

I watched the guy swaying around to the music and thought, 'Here we go. This has to be what it's like on a cruise ship.' I couldn't wait to get Ragsdale's take on the whole scene. The music dropped a notch and the guy spoke.

"Good evening. I am Chris Burner." Again somebody in the audience whistled. "And we are going to have some fun," he added. More applause and the music came back up.

The keyboard guy went straight into playing the opening to *New York, New York*. When the man started singing, my first reaction was that I don't think that I've heard a voice like this since my radio days and the late singer Lou Rawls. Wow!

In a matter of seconds, people were getting up from tables and moving to the small dance floor. At our table, Louie's smile almost matched that of the singer.

"Who'da thunk?" he said. I held my hands out and gestured toward Mr. Chris 'Da' Burner as though I had just introduced him. And that he would be appearing soon at a club near you.

With the music, conversations all around the restaurant got louder and the general room noise climbed a few decibels. Fortunately, the speakers were not blaring and we weren't seated close to them. We watched people dancing and the movements from the rest of the crowd. More customers were now coming in from the boats. I looked over toward the bar. Romey was nowhere in sight, but the other bartenders were moving right along. A couple of the waitresses were hustling with trays and taking drinks to tables.

A few feet away from the entrance, on the walkway between The Tipsy and the main office for the resort, Romey listened to the voicemail.

She put the phone to her chest, looked back at the crowd and all of the activity around the bar. Holding the phone face up, she tapped the screen and played the message again.

Thirty Seven
No Police

After pulling a gun from his jacket, Joey had ordered Mirella and Atty to move to the sofa. He pointed with the gun for them to be seated. He remained standing, leaning against the door, arms folded, gun in his right hand.

Atty went quiet, not looking at Joey or Mirella. She'd seen him do this before, a mannerism where he shifted his gaze from object to object all around a room, at the ceiling, at the floor, to the windows, never looking at any person close by. It was as though by avoiding eye contact with anyone in the room, Atty thought somehow that they couldn't see him.

At first, Joey watched Atty. Then he turned his attention to Mirella. She still had the defiant look but had not said anything more after the gun came out. Legs crossed, arms down with her hands resting on her thighs, Mirella did not give the appearance of being frightened. No one spoke.

Joey suspected that Terrence Williams likely owned a weapon and that this was not his wife's first exposure to a handgun. If there was a gun in the house, odds were that it was somewhere in the bedroom. There were two smaller bedrooms at the end of the hallway. Looking in that direction, Joey remembered Mirella and Terrence's son, TD, Junior, who was only a little younger than Atty.

"Where is your boy?" Joey asked. At first, no response from Mirella, just the look.

"He be helpin' his pop? Atty say Terrence fishing on Eluthera. That where your boy is, helpin' wit da boat?" Joey waited for an answer. Mirella shifted her hands from her legs and clasped them together in front of her. She looked at Atty, then back at Joey.

"TD is visiting his girlfriend," she said. Joey nodded.

"I *see* him wit dat girl. In Murphy Town. She older dan your boy." No reply from Mirella. Atty stole a sideways glance at his sister, then resumed exploring the room as if it were his first time there.

Joey pushed himself off the door frame and stepped forward, dropping his arms to his sides and the .38 pointing at the floor. With his left hand, he pulled a phone from the other jacket pocket and looked at it. He swiped his thumb across the screen, did it again, then put the phone back in the pocket. He looked at Mirella.

"Atty be tellin' you some trouble we have wit some bad boys from Haiti?" Joey said. Mirella jerked around and looked at Joey dead on when he said this, then slowly turned to look at her brother, who was staring at the window.

Joey moved in front of them and sat on the arm of the

sofa, closer to Atty. He reached over with his left hand and patted Atty on the top of his head.

"It is OK. Nobody goin' to get you," Joey said with a laugh. "No police, no voodoo men. Dey don't know where you live." He patted the head again, then pulled his hand back. Atty was now looking at the floor.

"And nobody goin to get Joey," he added, standing from the sofa. He looked at his watch.

"I be leavin' Abaco for good. Tonight." He stood over Atty and Mirella. For the first time since the gun appeared, Atty stared up at Joey.

Joey went across the room and dropped back to his slouch against the door. No words from anyone for several minutes. Joey mostly watching Mirella, Atty back to scanning the room. Then Mirella moved forward and sat on the edge of the sofa.

"I would like to go to the bathroom," she said. Joey stared at her. He again processed the thought of a weapon somewhere in the house. It would not be in the bathroom.

Making a point of squeezing her legs as though she was in discomfort, Mirella added, "Please. I really have to go."

"Don't be tryin to climb out a window," Joey said. "I will be here for only a few hours, den I'm gone. No police, no trouble. Everyone gonna be all right."

Mirella had gotten up from the sofa, hesitated, then started for the bathroom. Joey stepped behind her.

"You go for five minutes," Joey said. "Longer dan dat,

it will not be good." He looked back at Atty, then added, "For anyone."

Thirty Eight
Please Help

Holding the phone outside the bathroom window, leaning out so she couldn't be heard, Mirella made two quick calls, whispering rapidly into the phone.

The first call was to Terrence. No answer, straight to his voice mail. 'This is Terrence Williams, Abaco Bonefish Guide. Please leave a message.'

"Terrence," she said. "Joey Aberle is here. He has a gun. He say that he will be here for a few hours, then he is leaving Abaco." Mirella gulped, then went on. "I am afraid that he will hurt Atty. I think they be involved with dat shooting. The men who stole the boat. Joey threatened me. He says 'no police, nobody will be hurt'. I believe him. Please come home."

As soon as she clicked off the call to her husband, Mirella found Romey McIntosh in her contacts and placed the next call to her. Once again, directly to voicemail.

"Romey. A friend of Atty's is here at my home. A very bad man. He has a gun. I'm in the bathroom. He is threatening us. Told me that he will be here for a few hours, before leaving Abaco. I am afraid he will hurt Atty. Do not call the police. He will shoot us. I need your help."

Terrence Williams sat drinking beer with two other guides. The long boat trip from Marsh Harbour to Eluthera was not something that he would normally undertake. But repeat clients from Great Britain who had always been generous to him, they would give a good tip and pay all of the expenses, had persuaded him to make the three-day excursion, which included a stop for a half-day fishing on the flats of Spanish Wells.

The two English sports were fished out and most likely already in bed. It would be a long trip back tomorrow. Terrence was in top physical condition for a man of forty-six. He could handle just about anything, loved being on the water, liked most of the clients and always worked hard for his money. Now, relaxed for the first time since leaving home 36 hours ago, he laughed at many of the stories being told by the other guides.

After having spoken with his wife, he plugged his phone in to charge and came over to visit with the younger guides. They knew Eluthera very well and he didn't. One more beer, then call it a night.

Jameson knew that as soon as he left The Mud, he would see Joey before the late night rendezvous and the boat trip away from Abaco. After that, more than likely, a quick visit to see *one* of the fourteen-hundred inmates at Her Majesty's Prison, Fox Hill in Nassau, would be his next order of business. Then, back to Port 'au Prince and get ready for the coming New Year.

Before leaving his nephew's hovel, Jameson coiled a thin, twenty-four-inch leather garrotte and placed it in his back pocket. He had arrived on the island with a knife, as well. No guns, not here. The Bahamian government was widely known for a recently intensified effort to confiscate all illegal firearms. Back in Haiti, none of the guns that Jameson owned were legal.

Mirella hid the phone under some bath towels, flushed the toilet and opened the bathroom door. Joey was standing there, waiting, with his phone to his ear. Atty was still on the sofa.

Using the gun to motion for Mirella to be seated again, Joey was listening, not talking. He kept the phone pressed to his ear and followed Mirella. She sat next to her brother and patted his knee. Atty turned his head away from her.

"Hold on, mon," Joey said, holding the phone at arm's length and looking at his watch; 6:49. The .38 was still in his right hand. He looked at Mirella.

"You have sometin' to eat here? I will be stayin til ten o'clock," Joey said.

Thirty Nine
Have Fun Tonight

Inspector Denny Ring wanted to dance. Apprehensive about how it might play if he were to invite Cynthia Knowles onto the dance floor, he waited a minute. As a teenager, Denny's older sister had made him dance at home when she played music on the radio. And he knew that he was a good dancer.

In recent years his work with the RBPF had not allowed many opportunities to 'get down'. Now that he thought about it, almost from the minute the music had started when they had arrived at The Tipsy, he was pretty sure that his hang-up was more about how fellow officers might view him than the weak excuse about an absence of places to go to dance.

Knowles had teased him earlier about teaming up for a little Junkanoo dancing. The bright costumes worn by the dancers competing against other teams were usually more than a lot of *men* were willing to consider. But the guys who did it often stole the show.

The RBPF group was enjoying pizza, beer and soda like the other patrons. With the exception of Constable

Roos, they were in casual clothes and they were off duty. No, Ring didn't think that he could ask any of the other women to dance. No, he was not likely to get up there if they suddenly switched to a slow number. Yes, he was guaranteed to get some hoots as soon as his colleagues realized that he was going to dance.

As soon as the next song began, this singer's cover of Ringo Starr's cover of *Your'e Sixteen*, Denny tapped Cynthia Knowles on the shoulder and pointed at the dance floor. At first it didn't register. When he stood up and pointed again, she got it. Knowles face broke into a smile, she got up from her chair and was moving her arms to the music before they got to the dance floor.

Chris Burner worked the room, moving from the front of the stage out to the other side of the dining area next to the pool. The hand-held mic allowed him to invite audience members to join in at predicable spots during the songs.

One man, who appeared to be in his late thirties, danced with a young girl of nine or ten, most likely his daughter. The man was OK, the little girl was really good. And *really* enjoying the attention. Some people stayed on the dance floor for each number, others left or joined the dancing when a new song began. Some just needed a breather and came back out later.

The younger man at the keyboard got up and left the stage for a few minutes. Canned music was now playing, much like what takes place at a Karaoke event. When the keyboard player came back, the singer joined him once again and went into a new number.

Bartenders and waitresses, cooks at the pizza ovens, staff behind the buffet table, *all* were fully engaged in making this an enjoyable evening. Some of the staff from the resort had arrived and were gathered under a party tent off to one side. Out in the parking lot, a cluster of young boys on bicycles watched. People nearly a block away at the grocery store and some nearby residents could all hear the music.

Throughout the dining area, along the apron around the pool, and extending out to the boardwalk along the marina and in between the boats tied up, people of all ages, colors and sizes, and from different countries, were enjoying Abaco's 'Largest Social Event.'

Forty
Oldie But Goody

I nearly dropped the pizza that I was eating. Holding the slice in mid-air, I looked at Chris Burner, the singer up front, then looked at Ragsdale. Louie raised his eyebrows and held his hands up. What gives?

The guy with the keyboard mixer came right in with a combo of pre-recorded strings and percussion, built up the intro and led his vocalist to the opening of the song, *You'll Never Find Another Love Like Mine*. Too much of a coincidence.

"That is unreal," I said.

"What?" Louie asked. He looked at me, then at the singer. I put the pizza back on the plate, shook my head and laughed, then wiped my mouth with a napkin.

"When that guy started singing when we got here, my first thought was how much he sounded like Lou Rawls. Now listen to him." Becky stopped eating her salad. All three of us were watching the singer. Two older couples went out to the dance floor to join the others.

Louie held up his half-full bottle of Kalick, looked at it, took a long pull and put the bottle down next to his pizza.

187

"Summer, 1976, I think. Not sure that it made it to number one, but Rawls got some Grammys along the way," Louie said. Becky looked at her husband, then turned to me.

"I keep telling him that when he actually retires, he should go back and do an oldies show again." She touched Louie's right hand and added, "Some station would hire you."

"I don't *think* so," Louie responded. "Already did my part, thank you."

Chris Burner was really getting into the song and the crowd was definitely into him.

"Hey, maybe one of those community low power FM stations," I said. "Surely you've got one of those up there in the woods, huh?" Louie shook his head.

When I looked back at the singer, I saw Romey moving through the crowd. She appeared to be headed for our table. No drinks tray, serious expression on her face.

After checking the lines on his boat, Terrence Williams was ready to get some rest. The room was simple and functional; a single bed, small refrigerator, a coffeemaker and a table with two chairs, one of the basic rooms available for no-frills fishermen and boaters.

He pulled off his shoes, removed his shirt and pants and laid them over a chair. He removed the wallet from his pants and placed it next to the boat key on the table. His phone was right there where he'd left it two hours earlier, turned off, still charging. He turned out the light and fell asleep in seconds.

Mirella sat on the sofa watching Joey finish the food

she'd given him, reheated leftover stew from two nights earlier. Joey was a slurper. The sound was just one more irritant. Atty declined a bowl of the stew. He shifted nervously on the sofa sitting next to Mirella.

"Why you have to stay here?" Mirella said. "Atty is not going with you," she declared, again offering up her best look of defiance. Atty turned to look at her, but said nothing.

Joey slurped again and put down his spoon. He returned Mirella's stare for a few seconds, placed the empty bowl on the floor next to his feet and pulled the gun from his jacket, placing it on his lap.

"Atty say he wan' to go wit me. Dat is right, Atty? You not be stayin' Marsh Harbour for da rest of your life, no?" Joey laughed after he said this.

Before Atty could respond, Mirella stretched out her left arm in front of Atty as though she expected him to jump up at that moment.

"Atty be staying right here," she said, dropping her hand to Atty's knee. He looked at his sister, then at Joey.

Joey got up from the chair, pulled out his phone and swiped a thumb across the screen. He stared at the phone, then put it back inside the jacket.

"We not worry 'bout dat right now," Joey said. "Jus stay right here. Nobody leavin for awhile."

Forty One
Come With Me

Romey's smile was surprisingly restrained. In contrast to nearly every other person in the place, she looked like a school teacher about to admonish one of her rowdy second graders. She leaned in close and whispered to me.

"Could we talk, please?" I looked at her. Not sure what I might have said or done, my sense was that she was not happy at all, maybe with me, maybe with her boss, maybe the crowd and the noise level.

"Sure," I said. I pushed my chair away from the table. Becky and Louie both watched, but I couldn't tell if they got the vibe from Romey, who had now abruptly turned and was making her way back through the crowd.

"Back in a minute," I said. Ragsdale gave me a thumbs-up. Becky simply arched her eyebrows. Up front, Chris Burner broke into *My Cherie Amour*. More people moved onto the dance floor.

Just beyond the main entrance where people were still lining up to order pizza, a small canopy tent was located off to the side. Romey walked in that direction.

There were some empty folding chairs and two women, both wearing the floral print shirts indicating that they worked for the resort, sat in a corner talking to a man who was standing. He was dressed in khakis similar to those that I often wear, but he also wore the floral print shirt. Strapped to his belt was both a cellphone and a walkie talkie. He also wore tinted glasses. And he looked familiar.

Moving beyond the tent, Romey stopped at the walkway leading out to the parking lot. She turned and waited for me, clutching her phone with both hands. When I got there, the expression clearly conveyed that she was anxious about something. She looked directly at me without saying a word.

"What's up?" I said. No reply. Any previous smile or the light in her eyes was now replaced with what could only be described as concern.

"Romey, tell me what's wrong." She took a deep breath and shifted the phone, bringing it up to her chest.

"I have a friend who is in trouble," she said. She glanced over my shoulder at the three people still under the canopy, then looked down at her phone.

"A man has a gun. He is at my friend's house and is threatening her," she added.

I instinctively looked across the parking lot at the lights and houses in the village, then back to Romey.

"Here?" I said. "Or out where you live?"

She shook her head and hesitated.

"No. She lives in Marsh Harbour."

"Did you call the police?" As soon as the words were out of my mouth, I remembered that Romey's cousin and the other RBPF officers were back inside. I'd seen them on the dance floor as we came out.

"No. He told Mirella 'no police' or someone will get hurt. She's afraid he will shoot her brother. He is there with her." I stared at her without responding and she continued.

"Mirella Williams, she works here." Romey gestured toward the main office on the other side of the lot. "She was going to bring her brother here this evening. But she left a message on my phone."

"What exactly did she say? Does she know the man?"

Romey brought her phone up and tapped the screen. She held the phone close to my left ear.

"... a friend of Atty's is here at my home. A very bad man. He has a gun. I'm in the bathroom. He is threatening us. Told me that he will be here for a few hours, before leaving Abaco. I am afraid he will hurt Atty. *Do not* call the police. He will shoot us. I need your help."

Romey pulled the phone back.

"She said the man is a friend of Atty. Is that her brother?" Romey nodded.

"Yes. He has some problems. Mirella and her husband are trying to help him."

My immediate thought was drugs. Good chance that the guy threatening them was a dealer. Or, a desperate buyer.

"Does she know this man's name?" I said.

"I don't know. Maybe. She jus' say a friend of Atty."
We stood looking at each other. She really was frightened.

"You gotta tell the police," I said.

"No!" she said, taking hold of my arm. "You do not know how these men are. He will shoot them. It does not matter if the police get him after he has already killed someone."

Now it was my turn for the deep breath. She was still holding onto my arm. I took her hand away, held it in both of mine and looked right at her.

"Romey. What do you want me to do?"

Forty Two
Watching

Jameson and Clancy were standing outside the blue house. The plan was that they would walk to the neighborhood near the Marsh Harbour docks. Clancy would go off to get the raft, then return, while Jameson would stay back and wait.

It was hours before anyone would be leaving the beach to get on a boat. But Jameson had had enough of the squalor of The Mud and he had gotten all of the information that he expected to get. Now he wanted to resolve the issue with Joey Aberle, sooner rather than later.

"Dis mon, Joey. You know dat he be havin trouble wit police before?" Jameson said.

"I doan know dat. He come around sometimes. I seen him wit others," Clancy said. "Here in da Mud. And uptown in Marsh Harbour."

"He say he never been in jail. But you doan now if dat is true?" Clancy shook his head.

"No, mon."

Satellite photos showing a nighttime view of cities with populations of merely a few thousand, especially with sparse density, would provide only the tiniest of pen-point lights that reflected up from a small peninsula on the southwestern edge of Great Abaco Island. The small port area and docks of Marsh Harbour would be hard to detect.

Then again, unlike a constellation of military satellites continuously watching hotspots around the globe, it is hard to imagine that a camera from outer space would focus on this one small spot in the Bahamas.

If the weather satellites out there *were* taking periodic shots and sending back photos and other data, two men walking on a street in the dark were not only safe from any 'eye in the sky', it was also unlikely that their presence would attract the attention of the rare police patrol car. And it was *highly* improbable that there were any drones around, unless somebody on one of the boats in the marina had one and had nothing better to do.

While there are security and closed circuit TV cameras throughout the country, primarily on the more populated and developed islands, video surveillance on the out islands is more scattered. In Marsh Harbour, it is not a big concern, either for good citizens or the bad guys.

Jameson and Clancy kept walking.

Joey settled into the chair. The .38 was in the right pocket of his jacket, his phone was in his left hand resting on his lap. He gave occasional glances at Mirella and Atty seated on the sofa. Most of his attention was concentrated on the phone. Watching, waiting.

Following previous conversations with Jameson and the tension he felt after the most recent one, Joey grappled with taking the next step. He knew that it was unavoidable and necessary, knew the hours were growing short, and knew that once the step was taken, there would be no 'do over'. He just didn't know how he was going to do it.

Shooting the men who tried to cheat him after a bargain he'd struck and the risk that he had taken to steal a boat for them, that had been a reflexive action. Had he not shot them, *they* would have shot him. Simple. He didn't need time to ponder that choice.

On his walk to the Williams' residence, Joey had imagined a game board from his youth when he used to play checkers with his grandfather. As he grew older and got better at the game, his grandfather had always reminded him that even with a bad move, he still needed to *react* and consider his next move.

Being consumed for days by the fear of being arrested had significantly increased the desperation of wanting to leave the island. Both the need and the time for Joey to make that next move was now here.

Forty Three
Security

Romey was looking past me. She pulled her hand away, stepped forward, stopped, then turned back and took my left hand in hers.

"I would like for you to meet someone," she said, looking at me as she gently tugged me toward the canopy and the three people we'd seen when we came out. We walked in that direction. The two women and the man were still in conversation, one of the women doing the talking, maybe telling a joke, while the other two laughed.

"Reggie," Romey said. The man turned around. Now I placed him.

"Hey, Romey. Why you not working tonight? Dat is a good crowd," he said. She beckoned him with her right hand. He walked over to us.

"This is Michael Hanlon," she said, gesturing to me. "Michael, this is Reggie Sayle. He works with our security staff here at the resort."

She didn't know that I had used Reggie's taxi to meet the Ragsdales at the airport. Now sizing him up again, I figured he stood about five-nine and weighed maybe one-seventy-five. I had already guessed his age to be late fifties, possibly sixty or so.

"We met a few days ago," I said. "Reggie, how are you?" We shook hands again. Same firm grip, confident, easy smile.

"Yes, nice to see you," he said. Romey looked puzzled.

"Reggie took me out to the airport to meet Louie and Becky's plane," I said.

"Das right," he said to. "I still have my taxi, Romey, you know?"

She nodded, apparently now remembering his sideline business. Then she motioned for us to step away from the canopy and the two women. She turned to Reggie and placed her right hand on his chest.

"Mirella is in trouble," she said. He looked at her, then to me.

"Mirella Williams? What kind a trouble she be in? Not Terrence," he said. Romey shook her head.

"No. I think it is her brother, Atty. A man who knows the brother, he is at their home with a gun." Behind the tinted glasses, Reggie's eyebrows went up.

"She live in Marsh Harbour." It sounded like 'Mawsh Hawba'. Romey nodded.

"Where is Terrence?" he said.

"He is away guiding. Eluthera."

"Dat a *long way* to go for bonefish," he said.

Romey shrugged. "The man threatened Mirella not to call the police. He say he will shoot them."

Reggie was listening, eyes focused on Romey, as though he'd forgotten that I was even standing there. Romey continued with Mirella's story that the man had said that he planned to stay at the house until he was ready to leave the island. She pulled up her phone and played the voicemail for Reggie. He looked down at his feet while listening to the message.

"Is there someone here we can get to help?" she asked when the voicemail ended.

Reggie looked at his watch, a large-face analog style on a dark green nylon strap.

"I am off duty. I jus stopped to talk with Lori and Alicia," he said. No reply from Romey, but her eyes were pleading with Reggie.

"Will you go with us?" she said. "To Mirella's house?"

The sound and the pace of the music had slowed down. The vocalist and his keyboard partner apparently were taking another break. Lower volume, instrumental-only sounds came from the speakers, just one couple remained on the dance floor.

Becky and Louie were talking and it was a lot easier now to hear each other. Louie would spot someone's brightly colored clothing, or a particularly attractive woman, maybe some flamboyant behavior, then he would point it out to his wife and add editorial comments.

"Everyone is having a good time," Becky said. "For some people, part of that is wearing something they might not normally wear."

"Sure," Louie said. "Like her." He jerked his head to the right and gave a little point with his thumb that only Becky could see. She looked to see a woman in a very revealing, diamond blue sequin top, snug-fitting white slacks, and red shoes with three-inch heels. The woman was sashaying up to the bar. And she wore large gold hoop ear rings.

Becky laughed and hit Louie on the shoulder.

"I'll bet that she likes the way she looks," Becky said.

"No doubt," Louie replied.

Romey went back to the bar, had a brief conversation with one of the other bartenders, got her handbag and came back to where I stood. Reggie had gone to the main office. He'd said that he would meet us at his van in five minutes.

Looking across the room at Louie and Becky, I thought about the best way to explain what was about to happen. I was also trying to figure out how and if I should enlist Ragsdale to come along. My gut said no. Reggie knew the people of Abaco, knew the terrain and, I hoped, would know when to get the police involved.

All that aside, I also knew that I wouldn't bullshit Louie. I'd have to give him an idea of what was really happening and how I was about to become involved.

Romey came back out. Fascinating how a person's eyes can be so expressive. Hers now gave me the same pleading look that I'd seen a few minutes earlier when she had been talking to Reggie.

"Go find Reggie's van. It's a dark color. Maroon, I think. Has his name and phone number on the doors. I'll be there in a couple of minutes," I said, then turned and headed over to talk with Louie.

When I got back to the table, Becky was watching the dance floor and the other tables. I motioned for Louie to come over by the pool for a minute. He got up and followed me.

Forty Four
On The Road

"Let's not be stupid here, Hanlon," Louie repeated. He'd listened to my quick summary, interrupted me with a time out signal and 'don't be stupid', then listened for another minute. Now he was expecting me to listen and to pay attention.

"First sign that this ain't working, *call the police*," he said, emphasizing the words. After he said this, he turned and looked over his shoulder at the RBPF crew off on the other side of the room.

"Hey, for all I know, Romey's going to tell her cousin," I said but didn't really believe. Earlier I had hinted at that when she had first told me about Mirella, but she had rejected that and again stressed the plea for 'no police'. That's when she'd had the idea about talking with Reggie.

We went back to the table. Becky said that she was going to the ladies' room. Standing there for a minute next to the table Louie went quiet on me. His dead ass stare said enough. It was simply his way to put an exclamation point on 'don't be stupid.' Over time I had learned to interpret many of Louie's facial expressions. When we'd worked together in the past, it had taken me a while to decode some of the looks and the brevity of speech.

Reaching into his left front pants pocket, he pulled out his phone, held it up in front of my face and wiggled it, then tapped the phone twice with a finger.

"Call. Let me know what's going on."

"Yep." I turned to go to the parking lot. After two steps, I stopped and turned back to Louie.

"Hey," I said, reaching into a pocket of my shorts and pulling out a key on a yellow plastic twisty cord. I tossed the key and he reached up and caught it.

"The cottage," I said. He nodded.

Reggie Sayle placed his walkie talkie in a desk drawer, used the men's room, then called his wife. He told her that a work-related issue had come up, that he needed to make a quick trip to Marsh Harbour and that she shouldn't wait up for him.

His normal routine was in bed by 10 o'clock, up at six, maybe make a couple of taxi runs in his van each morning, then report to work at the resort from 11 am to 7 pm. One week a month it was reversed, when he worked the security shift overnight and then did any taxi runs in late morning and early afternoon.

Reggie had done a lot of things in his life and was a man of great utility, but this trip would be a new experience for him. At no time in the past had he been involved in something where a person had a gun and was making threats against others. That certainly had never occurred at the resort.

He left the security office, said goodnight to the young woman working the front desk and walked across the lawn to his van. Romey was there waiting, no sign of her friend.

"Tell me 'bout dis Michael Hanlon," Reggie said. She hadn't expected the question, was surprised at the flush she felt and hoped that Reggie hadn't noticed.

Romey looked away to see if she could spot Hanlon. Reggie waited for a reply.

"He is from Vermont," she said. "In the US."

"I know dis. We talked in my taxi when I take him to get his friends. I know where Vermont is," he added. "Close to Massachusetts. I spend some time in Boston many years ago. You know dis man for a long time?" She shook her head.

"No. Only since last week."

"What does he do in Vermont?"

Romey dug around in her purse, pulled out a business card and handed it to Reggie. He read the line *Private Investigation/Security Services*, then handed the card back.

"We had a conversation two days ago. He told me about a very unpleasant case. It is why he is doing this line of work," she said.

"Here he is," Reggie said, as Hanlon came walking across the parking lot.

There was no traffic on the highway heading south from TC. Romey sat up front with Reggie. I sat in the back on the left, behind Romey, so that I would have a better angle to talk with Reggie.

"It's my impression that all of the police in the Bahamas are part of the RBPF, you don't have local, independent police departments in each city or town." I said. Reggie was nodding in agreement with my assumption when Romey reached an arm across to him.

"No police," she said. He lifted his left arm from the steering wheel and held it up.

"Let us see what dis about," he said, glancing at her. "Is dis mon really dangerous? Is Mirella plenty scared only 'cause Terrence is not here?"

"When Romey told me about this, my first reaction was this is drug related," I said. "Mirella said that her brother knows the man."

"Dat could be. Too many young people be foolin' wit da bad stuff," Reggie said. "More dan jus young people," he added.

"Mirella has never told me anything about Atty and drugs," Romey said. "He has always had social problems with others, since he was very young."

"Doan mean cause she doan know dere is no problem," Reggie said.

My sense was that I would learn more by listening to these two hash it out in the front seat than by asking questions or making assumptions. They knew the people and the culture and I didn't. That old echo in my brain: never miss an opportunity to keep your mouth shut.

More talk about Mirella, about Terrence and how everyone knew him up and down Abaco and on the outer islands. Speculation about how things were different in Marsh Harbour because of more people, more tourists, illegal immigrants and so on. The patter between the two seemed to quicken and both of them dropped into the Bahamian dialect responding to each other.

"And den we have da mud," Reggie said. I'd seen a reference to 'The Mud' in a letter to the editor in *the abaconian*, but was unclear of the reference.

"What exactly *is* that?" I said. "The mud."

"It is where many Haitian refugees are living," Romey answered. "It is very crowded, no sanitary facilities. They say some shacks have animals and people living together."

"Da government has been trying to fix some tings," Reggie said, glancing into the rear view mirror. "It is not jus Abaco. Other islands have da same problem. Many people come here to Abaco, especially after dey have an earthquake. Or da hurricane las month."

Romey turned in her seat to face me. "Six years ago was the worst. More than a hundred-fifty-thousand people were killed. Over a million people lost homes. Since then, people from Haiti leave in boats all the time." She shook her head. "I have seen the news photos. You cannot believe how many are packed into the boats. Little children," she added.

She turned back around to face the windshield and the vast horizon on both sides of the highway, stars everywhere. They both went quiet for a couple of minutes. We were approaching lights and the scattered homes as we came into Marsh Harbour. Reggie was looking off to his right.

"Out there. Dat is da mud," he said. I looked that way. All I could see were the normal looking houses closest to the highway.

"Not all of dose people like what dey say in da paper. Some try to find work," he added, pronouncing it *woik*. "It is not good. Somtin' has to happen."

Forty Five
Slip Away

Jameson knew precisely how he was going to handle the departure. Before leaving the island there remained a question regarding an unknown quantity of cash that he believed to be in the possession of Joey Aberle. Where it had come from and how much there would be had not yet been clarified.

The money, depending on the amount, would be just an installment payment for Joey's escape. Their previous conversations had touched on this, but Jameson had purposely kept it vague. His suspicion was that a chunk of the cash had come from the two Haitians who'd been shot, two men very well-known to Jameson. He'd kept that information vague, as well.

One thing that was *not* vague was Joey's apparent sense of desperation. Whatever the amount of cash seemed to be only a partial concern. Jameson knew that before anyone left Abaco tonight, that concern would be cleared up.

The raft going out to meet the larger boat was the same raft that had brought Jameson ashore when he had arrived three days ago, also during the early morning hours. This Clancy was a busy man. Water taxi for late night arrivals and departures was a specialty service.

Jameson didn't kid himself that he was Clancy's first customer arriving from Port 'au Prince, nor was the nephew back in The Mud the only person who knew about Clancy and his business. It was one of the enterprises that functioned much better without a Bahamian Work Permit.

The surplus cash would be used more as insurance rather than a bonus for Clancy. It would help to offset any 'inconvenience' that might occur on this particular trip. They had yet to discuss the specifics, but during the walk to the docks Jameson had mentioned that some 'extra effort' might be called for. Clancy went with the flow.

With each passing minute, Joey became hyperactive. Up and down out of the chair, pacing, constantly checking his phone, going to the windows and the back door that opened onto the deck, getting a look at other houses close by. Twice in the last hour he had stood in the hall way while either Atty or Mirella used the bathroom.

It was 8:30. If they were going to slip offshore and board a vessel that would take them away, as Jameson had assured him that it would, he should be hearing any minute where and when. Joey believed that this kind of departure would not originate from the public boat access or the commercial slips along the marina. And it was not likely to leave from the ferry dock across town. It would be from some other spot.

Atty had fallen asleep on the sofa. Head leaning back, mouth open and his feet stretched out in front of him, he looked like he was fourteen, not twenty-four. Mirella had finally ceased the non-stop glaring. She was flipping through magazines, only stealing a glance every few minutes at Joey.

Deep in his stomach, as well as somewhere near the front of his brain, Joey felt a little connected tug of fear at the possibility that Terrence Williams would arrive home earlier than expected, maybe any minute. This caused him to keep checking the back door and the windows. Each time he did, he expected to see the big man coming to the house. Each time, so far anyway, he was relieved that the man was not there.

Romey had given Mirella's address to Reggie several minutes earlier, before they hit the outskirts of Marsh Harbour. Driving at a slower speed of 25 miles per hour, Reggie down-shifted as he turned off Bay Street and took a right hand turn onto Carleton Circle.

Four houses along, Romey pointed at a car just ahead on the left, parked next to a single story home.

"That is Mirella's car," she said. Reggie stopped the van and pulled to the side of the street.

Forty Six
Introductions

Louie Ragsdale decided that diplomacy was his best step. Ten minutes after Hanlon had gone from The Tipsy, and after a five-minute explanation to his wife, he rose from his chair and made his way across the room to where the RBPF group was seated.

Their crowd had thinned out some, now with just five of what he believed to be plain-clothes officers seated at two tables and a few empty chairs. The only member of the group who had arrived earlier in uniform, a younger man, was among those who'd left.

The woman, whom Hanlon had identified as Romey's cousin and who reportedly held the rank of Inspector, sat with four men. Hanlon had also told him that she was the one who knew Treasure Cay and was acting as the activity coordinator of the evening for her colleagues.

"Excuse me," Ragsdale said to the woman. She looked up and gave a polite smile.

"My name's Lou Ragsdale. I'm a policeman back in the US." He'd already thought about how he would handle this and had one of his police IDs ready, which he now handed to the woman. It showed a recent photo and said that he was assigned to the *Joint Northeast Counter-Drug Task Force*. The men at the table watched the exchange. The woman looked at the ID, then extended her right hand.

"Very nice to meet you. Inspector Cynthia Knowles, Royal Bahamas Police Force," she said.

As they shook hands, Ragsdale gave an informal, friendly glance and was careful to make eye contact with all of the others. The man seated next to Knowles gave a very casual, two-finger salute. Ragsdale recognized the fraternal, easy smile. He extended his hand and the man shook it.

"Ring. Like a telephone," the man said. "RBPF, Eluthera. I'm with her," he added, using his left thumb to indicate Knowles. She playfully pushed his hand back.

"Would you like to join us," Knowles asked, starting to get up from her chair. Ragsdale motioned for her to stay seated.

"Don't get up. I just wanted to say hello." Then Ragsdale sat in one of the empty chairs to Knowles' left. She straightened her posture, moved closer to the table, and began ticking off the names of the others. The music and crowd noise were still a distraction, but as each man was acknowledged by name, Ragsdale offered a combination of a slight nod and a wave.

"My wife and I are here with a friend. We met, I believe, your cousin, Romey?"

Knowles smile widened as she stretched to try and

see Romey somewhere over at the bar. She didn't spot her.

"Yes. Isn't she absolutely gorgeous?" Knowles said. "And everyone says that she is the best bartender on Abaco." She laughed, then added, "Of course, I am biased. But she is such a lovely person and has been my closest friend since we were children."

Ragsdale nodded. "She seems very nice. And thoughtful. She gave my friend, Michael, a tour out to the blue hole, then all the way to the end of the island."

"Yesterday," Knowles exclaimed. "We saw them. She stopped the car in Cooper's Town to say hello." Denny Ring was only half listening to the conversation. The other men were back to watching the dancers and the crowd. More people were now leaving after finishing their meal.

"Is your friend here?" Knowles asked, looking across the room.

"In fact, he's not. He's gone off with Romey."

Becky Ragsdale had spotted a woman she'd met while visiting a ceramics shop earlier in the week. The woman and her husband, the LeClairs, were visiting from Maine and were staying in one of the cottages. They'd just arrived at The Tipsy and were now coming to a table carrying one of the numbers that indicated that they had ordered pizza.

It had turned out the husband was a recently retired Maine state trooper. When Becky had learned this, she had told Lou about it and was eager for them to meet. Lou, on the other hand, had not shown a lot of enthusiasm about meeting someone with whom he would almost certainly wind up talking about law enforcement. He was on vacation, thank you. Besides, as he had reminded Becky, the fewer people who know him off duty, the better.

She had watched as the couple found a table, then got up and went to say hello and to meet the husband. Becky had quickly learned that this was their fifth time visiting Treasure Cay. Apparently there were several other couples from Maine and New Hampshire who frequently came to Abaco, according to Becky's new acquaintance.

"That's my husband, Lou, over there," Becky had said, pointing across the dance floor to where Lou was now seated and talking with some people. She'd no sooner said this when Lou and the woman he'd been talking with got up from the table. Becky watched as the two stood there talking.

Forty Seven
Let's Try This

During the drive from Treasure Cay, as had happened a few days ago, Reggie struck me as being a pretty laid-back guy. So when he shut off the engine, switched the lights to parking only and turned to face me in the back seat, I wasn't particularly surprised at what came next.

He studied me for a few seconds, removed his glasses and wiped them with a small cloth that he retrieved from the pocket of his shirt, then put the glasses back on.

"Michael. Do you mind tellin' me about da work you do?" he said. Again, *woik*, sounding more like wake. Earlier, I had heard him refer to a section of Marsh Harbor as *Moyfee* Town. I knew from my reading that it was actually Murphy Town. Reggie had a charming accent slightly different from most others that I'd heard since arriving on Abaco.

Romey turned around in her seat. She glanced at Reggie, then focused her gaze in my direction. She already knew a little about my work.

"Well," I began, "for the past couple of years, I've become active in what some people refer to as private investigation work. I'm not sure what you have here in the Bahamas, but much of what I've done, so far, is working for private citizens. I do *not* have any law enforcement background."

Images of a Maine State Police Lieutenant and some pretty unpleasant stuff, along with the memory of phone conversations and collaborating with police in Connecticut, trotted through my mind. I quickly amended my comments to Reggie.

"But I have had some success in working *with* the police. I'm not one of those guys who tries to avoid them."

Reggie nodded. "You say las' coulpla' years. What did you do before dat?" he said. Romey gave a faint smile as she and I had discussed a lot of this while having our picnic by the Sea of Abaco.

"I was a radio news reporter for a long time. Then I started my own company, working with small businesses, helping with marketing and some of the work they do in their communities." Reggie placed a hand on my knee and smiled, at the same time placing his other hand on Romey's shoulder.

"I am not being nosey," he said. "But, we gonna' do a little acting." He looked at Romey. "Dis be your new beau," he said. "You bringin him down heah to meet Mirella."

We listened as Reggie improvised a plan of how we were going to approach Mirella's front door, try to determine how serious the situation was inside, was there really a man with a gun, and, ask if Mirella would come have a drink to celebrate our engagement.

As soon as he finished saying this, Romey and I exchanged a 'what did you tell him?' look.

"While you at Mirella's front door," Reggie went on, "I will be at the back of the house." He paused to make sure that we were absorbing this.

"OK," I said. "We can do that. *But*, if there is a man in there with a gun and he doesn't buy this..."

Reggie held up his hand to interrupt me. "I will go to da back first." It sounded like *foist*. "You wait here for two minutes. Den you both go to the door. Knock and stand over to da side." He looked at Romey and added, "You say in a loud voice, Mirella, its Romey." He shifted his look from Romey to me. I nodded.

"Mirella comes to da door," he paused, eyes now shifting back and forth at each of us, "dis is when you gonna start *acting*." Now Romey nodded.

"When we knock, like you say, we'll stand off to one side. First sign that it's not a good situation, we're moving away from the house," I said.

"Das right," Reggie said, moving both hands in a pushing sideways motion. "Get away from da door." He turned, looked out at the other houses for a second, then added, "go between Mirella's house and da nex one."

"You want some kind of signal when you get to the back of the house?" I said. "I can give you a short, quick whistle." He shook his head and tapped his wristwatch.

"No. Jus wait two minutes. *After* you see me go back

dere," he pointed at the house. He started to open the driver's door, stopped and softly pulled it closed, turning back to me.

"If Mirella does not invite you in, or she be actin' scared, you leave and come back here." He tapped the steering wheel. "But if she tell you to come inside," he paused, again alternating the look at each of us, "pay attention for me to be knockin' at da *back* door."

Now Reggie stared only at me before adding, "When dat happens, we *all* be acting. So you stay loose, mon." He patted my knee again, opened the door and got out of the van.

Forty Eight
Stand By

Inspector Cynthia Knowles and Lou Ragsdale sat at the bar. The crowd had continued to dwindle as the dinner rush had peaked. The vocalist and keyboard duo were back on stage and several couples came and went to the dance floor depending on the music.

A female bartender stood across from them. Knowles didn't know the woman.

"A small glass of water, please," Knowles said. The bartender looked at Ragsdale.

"Kalick. Bottle, please." he said.

"Slice of lime?" the bartender asked. He shook his head. She went off for the drinks.

"Not trying to be mysterious here," Ragsdale began. "I know that you folks are off duty. But there may be a situation developing that you'll want to know about. I just didn't think that it would be a good idea to begin speculating there at your table." Knowles only response was a quick nod.

"By the way, you have an emergency contact number that the public can call, yes?" Ragsdale added.

"Always dial 919 in emergencies," she said with just the slightest smile. "It is posted everywhere you go. And our citizens do use it."

The bar stools were not the type that rotated when you turned, so Ragsdale stood up for a second to adjust his and to be able to look directly at Knowles. When he sat down again, he leaned his left elbow on the bar, arm raised with his hand closed to support his chin. He thought for a couple of seconds before he was ready to go on. Knowles took this all in without comment.

"Romey apparently has a friend who's having an issue at her home," Ragsdale said. "She called earlier, left an anxious voicemail."

The bartender returned with a clear plastic cup of water with ice and the bottle of beer. Romey thanked her. Ragsdale took a sip of the Kalick and put the bottle down on the bar.

"What did she mean that she was having an 'issue,' Knowles asked. "Did she say what it was about? Something with her husband. Or a boyfriend?" Again, Ragsdale hesitated. He and Hanlon had not discussed the possibility of an estranged husband or former boyfriend. Louie knew that many domestic conflicts at a private home could go south in a real hurry. He shook his head.

"No, I don't think so. My friend, Michael, who's with Romey, he heard the voicemail. He gave me the impression that the woman is home with a younger brother. The husband is off fishing, guiding, I believe."

When Knowles heard this, she turned her head away for maybe three seconds, then turned back to Ragsdale.

"Is the friend's name Mirella?" Knowles asked. Ragsdale was surprised.

"Yeah. I think that *is* the name Michael used."

"Mirella Williams. She works here," Knowles said, gesturing with her hand out beyond the crowd. "Her husband is a bonefish guide, Terrence Williams."

"OK. If you say so."

"I know Mirella. I used to work here before I joined the police." The tone in Knowles voice was showing a little agitation.

"Officer Ragsdale, you know something more than just a 'situation'. *Why* would Romey and your friend feel the need to go to Mirella's home?"

"Actually, they went with a man who works here in security. Reggie ..."

"Reggie Sayle," Knowles finished for him. "Yes. I know Reggie."

Ragsdale was thinking that he'd stalled just about as long as he could. He took his phone out of his pants pocket and placed it on the bar.

"Hanlon's going to call to let me know what's going on," he said. She watched him for a minute.

"But you felt the need to come over and get me and tell me all of this? Why not wait until you knew what is going on? Why didn't Romey come speak with me?"

"Apparently her friend begged her, no police."

222

Knowles picked up the plastic cup and took a drink of the water. She held the cup with both hands, took a second swallow, then carefully placed it back on the bar. She stared at Ragsdale's phone. "I believe this is all just a little strange," Knowles said. She watched Ragsdale for a response, but he said nothing. She shook her head, put both hands on the edge of the bar, pushed back and slid off the stool, then stepped away from the bar.

Before leaving, she placed her right hand on Ragsdale's arm, not a grip, but firm. She pointed in the direction to the tables where her colleagues were still seated.

"Perhaps it is nothing." A look. "Maybe something like this has happened before and Romey knows all about it," Knowles said.

"Maybe," Ragsdale echoed, although he didn't believe that.

Knowles looked down at the bar and pointed a finger at his cellphone.

"Will you please come tell me what you hear from your friend?" He gave a quick, silent nod.

Forty Nine
Not Yet

Jameson leaned his back against a coconut tree. He sat alone in the dark. When Clancy returned with the raft they would have plenty of time before the boat came for him.

Across the horizon to the west, off to the south, behind him to the east, and over his shoulder to the north, a dark sky full of stars, along with the occasional blinking lights of airplanes. His neck was beginning to ache from watching the sky. He rolled his head and shoulders.

All of the planes were coming from the US, out of Florida somewhere he believed, and heading for Santo Domingo, or San Juan, not Havana. Then he recalled that he'd read about a change, that the US had recently lifted their travel ban. Maybe the Yankee capitalists *were* going to Cuba?

Standing to stretch out the stiffness in his back and legs, he looked at his watch. It wasn't time. He would wait to call Joey. Taking a few, easy steps toward the seawall that he could see ahead of him, Jameson slipped his right hand into a back pocket to feel for the garrotte.

Joey Aberle resumed the nervous pacing. He'd just checked the windows and the back door to the deck again. Nothing.

Walking back and forth in this small living room, he kept his eyes on the phone in his hands giving only sideways glances at the two people on the sofa. Atty was still asleep, his sister now had her legs curled up and appeared as though she might fall asleep, too.

Absent mindedly, Joey slipped his hand into his pocket to feel the gun. It was warm from carrying it inside his jacket and having it in his hand earlier. It had been nearly two weeks since he'd shot the Haitians. He could still see both men, one going to his knees, the other pressing his hands to his abdomen and stepping backward. Atty had already started running, Joey had grabbed the remaining cash and followed.

He looked back at the sofa. He would have to waken Atty, get him to come outside.

Reggie went between two houses, staying low and close to the wall of the yellow, one-story house that Romey had identified as the Williams home.

Slowly and deliberately moving his head from right to left, then back again, Reggie looked for signs of movement or human activity inside either house. Two quiet steps, stop, wait, two more steps. Nothing.

At the corner of the house, his back pressed against

the siding, he saw a small wood deck with two molded plastic chairs and one single step that led down to the tiny back yard. The deck was 6 x 8 at the most, not much room. There was a glass sliding door and two small windows, all closed. Attached to the building next to the sliding door was an outside light fixture. The light was on but illuminated only small area, mostly the deck.

Eyes on the other house opposite from where he stood, Reggie crouched and moved closer to the deck. He could see the room inside, saw the back of a sofa and saw Mirella seated at one end. At the other end was a man with an arm resting on the back of the sofa, head tilted back. Must be asleep, or drunk and passed out. If he was dead, Mirella would not be sitting next to him.

Reggie looked at his watch. Almost two minutes had passed. He tip-toed onto the deck, back tight against the building, and moving as quietly as possible. He stopped and moved his head just enough to get a better view of the interior. That's when he saw the other man, not far from Mirella. The man was tall, walking slowly, head forward and staring at a phone that he held in his left hand about chest high. The man's right hand was inside the pocket of his jacket.

Fifty
Stay Awake

As soon as we saw Reggie disappear between the houses, I checked my watch; twenty of nine. I sent a quick text to Ragsdale, 'So far, so good.'

We sat in silence for another minute, both watching the house. Lights on somewhere inside, no windows near the front door and no movement that we could see.

"OK," I said. "Let's go." Romey opened her door, I pushed the handle to slide my door open and we got out of the van.

"Let's pretend like we're talking for a minute. When I say OK again, you point at the house. I'll go first. When we get to the front door, just like Reggie said, we'll stand off to one side." I glanced up at the door, then added, "We'll stay on the left." Romey nodded.

"Make it a loud knock. Like you're in a hurry. Then, let Mirella know that we're here."

Romey stepped away from the van and looked at all the other houses. She half-turned, then faced me.

"What kind of pizza did you have?" she said. I looked at her.

"What? What kind of pizza?"

"The topping, yes. What did you get?" She motioned with her hand for me to answer, as in, 'Come on, dummy. Pretend that we are *talking*.' I thought for a second.

"Black olives, onions, tomatoes and mushrooms."

Romey got closer, gave me a soft, very sweet kiss, stepped back and looked at me, then pointed at the house.

"I didn't say OK." She shrugged.

"OK," I repeated. She pointed again and we started for the house.

Mirella was fighting off sleep. Things had been mostly quiet since she'd fed Joey the leftover stew. Now he resumed the pacing back and forth. Atty had been asleep for almost an hour.

She had gone to the bathroom twice since Joey arrived, once when she made the calls and hid her phone, the second time when she really had to go. It was too soon to try that again. She would wait a while longer, tell Joey that she had been having a bladder problem and that she really had to pee. Use the phone again. Call TD, Junior.

Joey stopped walking, looked at Mirella, then sat down on the floor and leaned his back against the wall.

He placed his phone on the floor next to him, raised both arms high over his head and held his hands together, much like a fighter who'd just been declared the winner of

228

the bout. Then he lowered the arms, stretched them in front of his body, moved them slowly back and forth twice and dropped them. His hands were in his lap, fingers laced together and resting between his legs, almost touching the floor.

All the time that Joey was going through this little exercise, Mirella watched him. He did not take his eyes off of her. Now they sat staring at one another. Finally, Joey averted his eyes and picked up the phone to resume staring at it.

The sound of knocking at the front door.

Fifty One
Wait

Reggie watched the man sitting on the floor looking at his phone. He heard the knocking and Romey's voice at the front door.

"Mirella. Are you home, girl? It's Romey." More knocking. The man pushed up from the floor, his right hand going to a pocket in his jacket and he pulled out a gun. The man was now looking at Mirella, then back to the front door. Romey's voice again.

"Hey, Mirella. I want you to meet someone," came from the other side of the door. Mirella shifted her legs from the sofa back to the floor. The man who had been passed out started to wake up. He looked at Mirella, then looked at the tall man holding the gun.

Reggie watched and waited, ready to move.

When the text message came in, Ragsdale decided not to approach Cynthia Knowles immediately. If things got urgent, he knew that Hanlon would call. Then it might be time to 'Dial 919.'

Becky came back from talking with the couple from Maine. She was not aware of what was going on with Hanlon and when she'd asked where Michael had gone off to, Louie had faked a story that he thought that Hanlon was at the main office with Romey, that apparently there was something that they needed to talk about. Hoping to make it sound more convincing, he did the kiss, kiss effect again. His wife rolled her eyes.

"You know, Louis James Ragsdale," Becky said, "a lot of men are not as lucky as you."

"And how is that?" He'd heard it before, but played along to see what his wife's retort would be this time.

"You got it right the *first* time. You picked me."

"Hmm." He scratched his right ear, then added, "And all this time I thought that *you* picked me." She leaned in, exaggerated batting her eyelids, then puckered for a kiss. Louie obliged.

Jameson was back under the coconut tree. He looked at his watch. Another twenty minutes and then he would call Joey. The walk to the docks would not take more than half an hour at the most.

In approximately forty-five minutes, Clancy would show up with the raft. If Joey wasn't here by then, they would wait a few minutes longer. What he had in mind would be resolved quickly.

Jameson knew that once they were on the boat, the trip could take up to three hours, putting them offshore from New Providence in the middle of the night. Then it would be another short trip, also by inflatable raft, allowing him to go ashore before daylight. He briefly reconsidered the question of how much money Joey had from his exploits. Really didn't matter.

But that led to the thought that visiting hours tomorrow at Her Majesty's Prison in Nassau would be from 10 to 4:30. Jameson would have his first face-to-face with the man who survived the shooting incident on Abaco. He hoped to clarify how long the man would be behind bars before being 'repatriated' to Haiti. He believed that the man had not given up information that would endanger others

Now fifteen minutes until the call to Joey.

Fifty Two
Move Fast

"Mirella, I want you to meet someone." Mirella sat up. It was Romey's voice. Atty came forward slowly and looked around. Joey shoved the phone into his jacket and held the gun with both hands.

Joey stepped toward the door. He listened. He pointed the gun first at Mirella, then at Atty. He motioned with his other hand for Mirella to come to the door. She didn't move. He motioned again more vigorously while at the same time aiming the gun in Atty's direction.   Mirella stood from the sofa and moved slowly toward Joey. When she was within reach, he grabbed her arm and pulled her close to him. He kept his right arm out straight and the gun on Atty.

"You say this not a good time," Joey whispered. She glared at him. "Say you not feeling well," Joey added, squeezing her arm and giving her a little jerk. They were both close to the door, Joey now moving behind Mirella and shoving her forward.

Reggie watched the man pushing Mirella toward the door. The man on the sofa had leaned forward, but showed no sign of going after the man with the gun.

Back pressed against the house, Reggie took another quick glance to see what the man would do. Mirella was now closer to the front door. She was saying something that Reggie couldn't hear.

Under the driver's seat in the van, Reggie had a Beretta 92 semi-automatic pistol in a leather holster. It was licensed to him for his work, though he hadn't fired the gun in more than a year. Security detail at a vacation resort had never required him to use the weapon and he never actually wore the gun on the job. He had cleaned it a couple of times during the year. It didn't matter, the gun was back in the van.

As softly as he could, Reggie stepped away from the door and off the deck, now he was moving low and fast back between the houses. He held up near the front corner, then let out a quick, short whistle.

As soon as Romey knocked the second time and told Mirella that she wanted her to meet someone, I pushed her behind me and we both stepped off to the left as planned. At first there no response. Now Mirella was saying something.

"Romea, I'm not feeling well," she said. "I am lying down for a spell. Come back in the morning. Okay?" I looked at Romey. She shook her head. I held up my hand

234

for her to remain silent. We waited to see if Mirella would say anything else, maybe open the door. Nothing.

Then I heard someone whistle. Had to be Reggie.

Backing away from the house and keeping Romey behind me, I saw him. He stood perfectly still, like a man size lawn ornament. I made a little sideways motion with my right hand flat to acknowledge that I'd seen him. He slowly raised his left arm and motioned with two fingers in a pointing gesture for us to go back to the van.

Walking fast, I looked around at the other houses and the vehicles parked near them. There had been no traffic on this street since we'd arrived. That could change in a second. I looked back at Mirella's house. I couldn't see if Reggie was still in place.

As soon as we got to the van, I opened the sliding side door. Both of us got onto the middle seat. Romey was shaking her head again.

"She never calls me Romea." Even with the dimness of the interior light I could see that her eyes were wide, nostrils flared and lips tight in a grimace.

"OK. We have to wait for Reggie," I said.

Fifty Three
Who is dis?

Reggie stood in place, taking slow, shallow breaths through his mouth. Hanlon and Romey were now back at the van. He saw the dome light come on and heard the click of the door closing.

No sound from the front of the house. He wished that Romey would have said something as she left, something to make the man with the gun believe that she was really leaving. Too late. A quick look at his watch. Just like the approach, he would wait a full two minutes before making his way back to the van.

Aside from the earlier thought about the Beretta under the seat, he knew that despite any arguments from Romey, they had just moved past the 'no police' option. He only hoped that the man inside had been fooled enough to believe that Romey and her friend had gone away. And he hoped that the man inside was not crazy, or easily prone to violence.

Joey had his left forearm against Mirella's chest, holding her against the wall. They both waited for a response from the other side of the door. None came.

"Joey," Atty said. Joey twisted his right arm around and aimed the gun. Atty continued staring at him. Joey raised the gun as though he were sighting it.

"You do not hurt Mirella," Atty continued. "She do nothin' to you."

Joey waggled the gun a couple of times, again pretending to take a dead aim on Atty, then he aimed the gun toward Mirella. He moved his arm away from her, but quickly grabbed her left elbow and shoved her back in the direction of the sofa. She stumbled, kept her balance, then moved to the sofa and sat where she'd been for most of the last three hours.

"Who is Romea?" Joey said. Mirella didn't answer. Joey took a step forward and waggled the gun again. "Who is dis woman?"

"She is a friend who works with me."

"In Treasure Cay?" Mirella nodded.

"Yes. At the resort," she said.

Joey backed up to the front door again, listened for several seconds, then took two steps toward the sofa. He looked at Mirella for any sign that she was lying.

"If she come back, we gonna' have a problem," Joey said. "If she not coming back," he nodded his head repeatedly, "dat be OK. No problem."

He moved to the back door and looked out, then to both windows. Just as he turned to face Atty and Mirella,

Joey's phone began playing some tune. He jerked the phone from his pocket and looked at the screen. Before answering he said, "I be leavin' here soon."

Joey put the phone up to his ear. "Yah, mon."

Reggie bent forward into a crouch and moved rapidly through the yard. When he got to the street, he straightened up and walked at a brisk pace. As soon as he reached the van, he got in behind the wheel, quietly pulled the door closed and turned to face Romey and Hanlon.

Nobody spoke for a few seconds. Reggie was breathing hard. Then Romey shook her head.

"This is not good. Somebody is there, jus like Mirella said when she called me." Reggie nodded. He pulled a handkerchief from a rear pocket, wiped his brow and his mouth, then put the handkerchief away.

"There is a man inside. Two men. One of them has a gun. He held it on Mirella when you were at the door."

"Two men?" Hanlon said. Another nod from Reggie.

"One of them is Atty, I believe," Romey said. "Mirella's brother."

"Dat could be," Reggie said. "He was asleep on da sofa, where Mirella was sitting."

"She never calls me Romea," Romey said. "She is scared."

Reggie picked up his phone from the console between the front seats. He was about to tap some numbers when Romey put a hand on his on his left arm.

"Who are you calling?" she said. "No police. Please. He will shoot them."

Reggie held the phone but did not place the call.

Fifty Four
All Boats In

"Past the end of the seawall, come up the beach," Jameson said. "No lights here. I will see you coming. Away from the docks, jus keep walking." Joey listened. The man had more to say.

"You have finished what you need to do? You are ready to leave Abaco?"

"Yes," Joey lied in answer to the first question. "Yes," he repeated, not lying about the second.

He'd been ready to leave for a long, long time. The shooting incident with the Haitians had only increased his desperation to get away from this island. On his last visit to The Mud, looking at the living conditions of so many people, he'd had a brief thought of what little he knew about earthquakes and hurricanes and poverty that drove these people off *their* island.

"How long before you will be here?" Jameson asked. Joey looked at his watch.

"Soon. Fifteen minutes," he answered and ended the call, putting the phone back in his jacket and turned to Atty and Mirella.

Jameson had been watching the public ferry dock for nearly two hours. The last boat offloaded a small group of people just after 9 o'clock. The captain and two-member crew departed a few minutes later. The ferry was tied up for the first run the next morning to one of the outer cays.

On occasion, almost always during daylight hours, other privately-owned boats might pull in to this dock before going the short distance around to the marina located on the other side of the peninsula. Larger ferries, from Nassau and other ports, came in farther down at Sandy Point. No other boats had arrived here in the last hour.

The departure point for Clancy's raft would be more than two-hundred feet up the beach, at a low spot along the western side. There were few rocks near the shoreline and the run out to the boat would take just a few minutes.

Walking along the beach, Jameson again checked the sparsely wooded lot next to an unpaved parking area. He'd seen the only car parked there leave shortly after the last ferry docked. There were no houses near the wooded area. Clancy would be coming in the raft from the north, staying close to shore.

Looking at his watch, Jameson gazed up at the stars again. A quiet, clear night, only the sound of water hitting against the docks, the tide rolling softly in and out along the beach.

A good night to leave Abaco.

When Joey finished the phone call, Mirella tensed up. She knew that if he was really preparing to leave, this was the most dangerous time since he came to the house. How she wished that Terrence would come, that Romey would come back, that TD and his girlfriend would come by, that *someone* would help them.

Joey walked over to Atty and stood looking down at him. The hand holding the gun was relaxed and he held his arm down at his side, the gun pointing at the floor.

"Les go outside, Atty," Joey said. Atty looked up. He pushed himself up slowly from the sofa. Joey stepped back.

"What are you going to do?" Mirella said. She made no signs of getting up, but the alarm in her voice was clear. "Atty is not going with you," she added.

Joey looked down at her, moved the gun hand slightly but did not aim it at Mirella.

"We gonna' have a talk," Joey said. "Atty get to decide wha' he be doing."

Atty stepped in front of Joey and started for the front door. Joey took his right arm, pulling Atty back.

"No, mon." He motioned with the gun to the back door. "We go out back. Nobody see us talkin." Atty turned toward the back door with Joey behind him.

"Atty," Mirella pleaded. "You do not go with this man."

The second the door closed behind them, Mirella went to the bathroom and pulled her phone from underneath the stack of bath towels.

Fifty Five
Dial 919

Reggie rested his right arm on the steering wheel, holding his mobile phone. Romey still had a hand on his left arm. Neither of them spoke. I leaned forward and gently pulled Romey's hand back.

"Let's talk about this for a second," I said. Romey looked at me.

"Was the man with the gun acting like he would really *shoot* Mirella?" I said to Reggie, then added, "Did he just have the gun in his hand, or was he actually pointing it at her?" Reggie hesitated.

"When you were at da door, the man pull a gun from his jacket. He made Mirella go first, but he aim da gun at da other man. Da brother," Reggie said. "If da brother say something, I didn't hear it," he added.

"Was he threatening Mirella with the gun?" I asked again.

"No. He stay behind her at da door, but keep da gun on da brother."

"Then what?" Reggie shook his head.

"Dat is when I turn and move from da house," he

said. "I am hoping you and Romey move away, like we talk bout earlier."

Reggie still held his phone, ready to call the police. I looked at Romey.

"Romey's cousin and some other policemen were at The Tipsy when we left," I said.

"Dat is forty minutes away," Reggie quickly replied. "Dere be police right heah in Mawsh Hawba." I nodded in agreement.

"Got it. But, if we're going to call the police *here*, I say that we let the others know," I said.

"Yes," Romey said. "Cyndy would help."

"It is not a good idea to be formin' a committee," Reggie offered in a bit of a sarcastic tone. "Nothin' they know dat da boys down heah don't know."

"You're probably right," I said. I pointed at Reggie and added, "You call the police. Make sure that you tell them about Mirella's call to Romey earlier this evening, that the man told her 'no police.'

I pushed the handle to open the door and hooked my thumb at Romey for her to follow me. As soon as we were out of the van, I turned to her and held my left hand up to my ear to simulate using a phone.

"Call your cousin. Tell her what Reggie is doing." She pulled her phone from her hand bag, I got my phone out to call Ragsdale.

The ringtone app kicked-off with *Louie, Louie* and the distinctive guitar/keyboard intro before the vocal. Ragsdale answered his phone.

"Yes," he said, knowing that it was Hanlon. Becky watched.

"Hey. We're underway here. There *is* a guy with a gun. We went to the door. She wouldn't open it, said she wasn't feeling well. We're calling the cops."

"Where are you?"

"At Reggie's van," I said, turning around to look back at Mirella's house. "Maybe fifty yards down the street from the house."

"Reggie? The security guy with the taxi?"

"Yeah. He's on the phone with the police in Marsh Harbour."

"I had a word with the RBPF woman. Romey's cousin."

"Oh yeah? And told her what?" I asked.

"Nothing about what's going on. Just that there was a 'situation' and that you had gone off with Romey."

"What'd she say to that?"

"Not much," Louie replied. "Thanked me. Asked me to let her know if I heard anything."

"I'll call you back when we know what's happening."

"Sorry, partner. Not a lot I can do from here," he said. "Stay safe, be smart. *Listen* to the cops."

"Got it." I clicked off. Romey was still on her phone a few feet away from me. Inside the van, Reggie was still talking on his phone.

Inspector Cythina Knowles closed her phone, stood and turned away from the table. She looked across the dance floor at Lou Ragsdale and his wife. Ragsdale was getting up from his chair.

Turning back to face the other RBPF officers, Knowles leaned forward and tapped Denny Ring on the shoulder. He looked up. She got close enough for him to hear.

"There's an incident in Marsh Harbor. Man with a gun, maybe a hostage situation," she said. Ring sat up straight.

"My cousin Romey is there. She's with a security man from here at the resort."

"She's part of the situation?" Ring said, surprised.

"No. She knows the hostage. They're outside, away from the house. They just called it in to Marsh Harbor."

"You want to go?" Ring said, turning around in his chair.

"In a minute," she said. "I need to speak to the American drug cop." She looked back at Ragsdale, who was now coming in their direction.

"His friend is also there with Romey."

Fifty Six
Take Dis

Joey followed Atty out to the back deck. He tapped Atty on the shoulder with the gun, then pointed to the two plastic chairs.

Joey would take the next few minutes very carefully. He'd thought about how this would go from the moment when he knew that he would actually be leaving. Possibly never to return.

Atty lowered himself into a chair. Joey remained standing but put a foot up on the other chair. He casually rested both arms across his legs, the gun still in his right hand and pointed down. He studied Atty's face.

"It is time for me to be leavin Abaco. It doan make sense for you to go," Joey said.

"I want to go," Atty began. Joey held his left hand up for Atty to listen, not talk. He dropped his foot from the chair and sat in it, gun now resting on his knee. He stared at Atty.

"Dis mon takin me to Nassau, he doan *know* you. He will not be foolin wit people he doan know."

"I have some money," Atty said. He spoke rapidly,

247

voice high-pitched, almost sobbing. "You goin' to give me some money. Thas what you tellin me when dem boys be shot." Joey shook his head.

"Is not da money," Joey said. "Da mon have money. He wans me to do some work for him." He shook his head again. "He say jus one from Abaco," Joey tapped his chest with his left hand, "Me."

Atty shifted in the chair and looked away. Joey didn't think that he could deal with any whining or blubbering. Joey stood up again, with his left hand reaching into a pants pocket and pulling out a small wad of bills. He dropped the money on the deck at Atty's feet.

"Dis is yours," Joey said. Atty turned back to face him. Joey motioned with the gun at the money. Atty looked down, then looked back up. Joey nodded and jerked the gun again more emphatically.

"You take dis," he said.

Atty didn't move. Then, very slowly, he leaned forward in the chair, bent at the waist and reached down to pick up the money.

Joey raised the gun and came down hard and fast on the back of Atty's head. The blow hit in the back of the skull just behind his left ear. Atty fell forward onto the deck.

Joey watched him for a few seconds. Blood appeared where the gun made contact, a small trickle going down onto the deck. Kneeling, Joey felt for Atty's pulse. It was strong. Good. Joey was relieved. He will be out for a while, but he will be OK.

Mirella did not call Terrence again. If he'd heard her earlier voicemail, he would have called back and left some kind of message alerting her to where he was. And that he'd heard her message and was coming home. No, this late, Terrence was asleep, still on Eluthera.

Instead, she tried Romey's phone again. She was surprised when Romey answered.

"Mirella? Romey said.

"Romey. Joey Aberle is still here." She was speaking in a whisper. "He has taken Atty outside. Where are you?"

"We're still here, on your street. The police are coming," Romey said.

"No-o," Mirella cried. She caught herself, put her hand over her mouth and looked at the door. Nothing.

"He say that he is leaving. If the police are here, he will shoot Atty. And me," she was back to the whisper. "This man is no good. He is dangerous." Mirella closed her eyes, put a hand to her brow and lowered her head. She sobbed, right at the edge of losing it.

"Mirella, listen," Romey said. "Reggie Sayle is with us. He explained to the police what is happening. Reggie saw the man with the gun. The police will be careful. They know about things like this." No response. Romey went on. "Police don't want you or Atty to get hurt."

There was a loud thud against the bathroom door and

it flew open.

Mirella turned, moved the phone from her ear and saw Joey standing in the middle of the open door. When he saw the phone in her hand, he shook his head and stepped into the bathroom.

Fifty Seven
Change Fast

The white RBPF patrol car from Marsh Harbour stopped next to Reggie's van. No flashing lights, no siren, very little noise as the car pulled up. Large blue letters on the side, *POLICE*, and the red, circular RBPF emblem on the fender above the front tire. There were two officers in the car; the driver's window went down.

The three of us were back inside the van. Reggie opened his door and got out. Romey and I stayed where we were, sitting next to each other in the middle seat. She had just finished telling us about the sudden end to her phone conversation with Mirella and the name of the man with the gun. Reggie would give this new information to the cops.

I pulled the handle and opened the side door so that we could hear. The sound of the door sliding open caused Reggie to turn around. He held up his hand for us to stay inside the van. I motioned that I understood, we stayed put and he turned back to face the police car.

When Ragsdale reached the table, Inspector Cynthia Knowles was standing, waiting and looking directly at him. The other RBPF officers remained seated, but unlike the first visit across the room just twenty minutes earlier, all four men were now looking at him. He stepped closer to Knowles and placed his right hand on the back of a chair.

"Listen, I just had a call from Hanlon," he said. Before he could continue, Knowles interrupted.

"This is your friend Michael, yes?"

"Yeah. And he says ..."

"I already know. Romey called me. The police in Marsh Harbour are on the way." It took Ragsdale a second to process this, then he nodded. Of course she would call. Hanlon had called him. Why not?

"Are you going down there?" Ragsdale asked.

"Maybe," she said. "We have to go back to Cooper's Town." She slowly swiped both hands down the front of her shirt and slacks as if she were brushing off crumbs. "Look at us," she added, gesturing to the others, all dressed casually.

"If you do decide go to Marsh Harbour, probably not a chance that I might come along?"

Knowles pursed her lips tight and shook her head. "That would not be a good idea, I think."

One of the younger officers drove the van back to Cooper's Town. He hadn't been selected to be a designated driver, but he'd had only one beer and was OK with the role.

Ring and two other officers were in the back, Knowles in the front passenger seat on the left. She was on the phone with a corporal at the RBPF station in Marsh Harbour who told her that a second patrol car with two additional officers was heading out.

The two officers already there were in what he described as 'close proximity' to the house. As soon as the second car arrived, they would assess the situation and make their plan, most likely surrounding the house. There had not been any further communication with the woman inside.

"We are coming from Cooper's Town," she said, looking at her watch. "Five officers, one hour." She knew when she said this that getting into uniform, collecting gear, turning around and driving forty miles to the scene would be a real push. But it was nighttime, there would be little traffic on the highway. They could do it.

She ended the call, turned to the men behind her and appraised their condition and alertness. They looked OK. And ready.

"You remember your second year of training, Hostage Negotiation/Secure Perimeter?" Knowles asked.

"Communicate before advance," Ring said. "Everyone who goes through has trained for that." Both the other officers nodded.

"If we are fortunate, that is all we will be dealing with,

getting hostages released." She watched their reaction, turned back to face the windshield before adding, "If that is not the case, and there is shooting, *not* so fortunate." After a pause, she tacked-on, "And it could end badly before we get there."

The turnoff in Cooper's Town was coming up. They would change and have their gear back at the van in less than five minutes.

Reggie told us what was about to happen. We watched the two policemen, both with guns drawn, leaving the patrol car and going to opposite sides of Mirella's house. They stayed in the street away from the house.

"Another patrol car is on the way," Reggie said. "As soon as it is here, dey will woik a plan and surround da house."

No one had come out from any of the other houses. I hadn't noticed porch lights come on and had not seen anyone at a window. If a second patrol car showed up, that wouldn't last. I was sure that the Bahamian cops would have a way to deal with curious neighbors before things start to happen.

"When the other cops get here, are they planning to confront Joey what's-his-name? Try to force him to let Mirella and her brother come out?" I asked.

"Dat is probly what dey will do," he replied.

Romey was shaking her head. "If he shoots them, it will be too late," she said. I put my hand on her shoulder.

"If they hear shots," I said, pointing at the two policemen moving up the street, "I suspect things will change really fast."

"Les hope dere is no shooting before da other car gets here," Reggie said.

Fifty Eight
Confirmed Sighting

Joey jerked Mirella's phone from her hand, grabbed her other wrist and dragged her to the kitchen. She stumbled when he shoved her to the door so that she could see Atty, then let out a scream when she saw her brother face down on the deck.

Pulling her around to face him, squeezing and twisting her arm as though he might break it, Joey held the gun up to his right shoulder with it pointed at the ceiling. His eyes were bugged wide in anger, chin jutted out.

"Atty is OK," he shouted. "I jus knock him out so I can leave here. He is *not* goin wit me." Mirella was frightened of what Joey would do, but she was relieved that Atty was not dead.

"What do you want? Just leave," she said, trying to free her arm. Joey held on. He looked back at the bathroom door and pulled her in that direction. Then he released her arm, reached down and picked up the phone from the floor. He had the gun aimed at Mirella.

Joey looked at the phone. It was a very basic older model with no screen.

"You callin' da police?" he said. She shook her head vigorously.

"No! I was calling Mirella. The woman who was at the door," she said, pointing. Joey glared at her, looked at the phone, then shoved it into the same pocket that held his phone. He stepped toward Mirella and pointed the gun at her.

"You sit," he said, waving the gun toward the sofa. "Now," he yelled. Mirella backed to the sofa and sat where she'd been most of the evening. Joey's eyes shifted to the back door but he didn't move.

"I am getting Atty's phone. Den I be leaving. You do some ting, I shoot Atty and *den* I shoot you." He watched her as he stepped sideways to the back door, went out and came back quickly with Atty's phone in his hand. He stood in front of Mirella while he shoved Atty's phone into his pocket.

"Doan be dumb. You stay dere, do not move for five minutes until I am gone. Den you can help Atty. If you move, I will come back and use dis," he said, waggling the gun at her.

Joey began moving backward in the direction of the front door.

One of the patrolmen moving up Carleton Circle saw the door of Mirella's house open. He watched a tall man step out, look around, stop and look in the direction where he was standing. Then the man hurriedly went back inside

257

and the door slammed shut.

The officer crouched and began backing up. He then stood, went behind one of the houses on the opposite side of the street and hustled back to where his partner could see him. He motioned that they should return to the patrol car.

Jameson checked his watch again. Almost fifteen minutes since he had spoken with Joey. He should be here shortly. Clancy would be paddling the raft down to meet him in a few minutes.

Leaving the beach for the third time since he'd been waiting, Jameson stepped back close to the wooded area and stood next to one of the larger pine trees. As soon as Joey arrived and got close enough, he would step out so that Joey could see him, then he would wait.

There was one boat far out on the water heading north. He could see the bow lights and the stern light. The boat was moving at a good speed, but in the wrong direction. It was not the boat that would take him to Nassau.

Fifty Nine
Stay Here

Romey was more anxious now than she had been since first hearing Mirella's voicemail earlier. There was nothing that she could do, which only heightened her anxiety. Watching through the side window, waiting for more policemen to arrive, wondering if the RBPF officers in Cooper's Town were on their way. Romey leaned her head back and rested on the seat. She closed her eyes.

Reggie and Michael Hanlon were not talking. They watched the policemen through the windows. Michael had opened the side door just enough to have a better view. Nothing from the street, no other cars. She thought that she could hear what sounded like a television from inside one of the houses.

Her mind went back to when she and Mirella had first met. Both had been young and nervous about their new jobs at the resort. Mirella had been a lot more confident, though. She was older, married and had a little boy. At first she had worked only two days a week while her toddler stayed with Mirella's mother. When her son started going to school Mirella was able to work additional shifts.

Romey thought about all of the times they had laughed together, how Mirella had always made a point of coming to visit with her after Romey's job had changed and she became a bartender. All the times they had sat talking while on break. Mirella was a strong, good and caring person.

There was the sound of a car approaching. Romey opened her eyes and brought her head forward. She reached over and took Michael's hand.

I turned to look at Romey. She'd taken hold of my hand just as the second patrol car pulled in behind the first car. Again, no flashing lights.

I gave her hand a squeeze and inhaled deeply, holding the breath for a couple of seconds, then exhaling through my mouth. She looked at me, didn't speak, then turned to watch the policemen. Reggie opened his door to get out.

After a minute or so of Reggie talking with the four policemen, one of the officers who'd just arrived turned to look at the van. Reggie was still talking. Then a second officer, one of the first two on the scene, turned to look at us and stepped toward the van. As he approached, he beckoned for us to get out. I climbed out first, Romey came behind me.

"I am Sergeant Pinder. The woman inside the house is a friend of yours?" he said to Romey.

"Yes."

"When she called, she told you the man with the gun is Joey Aberle?"

Romey nodded.

"Do you know how this man is connected to your friend?" he asked. "Are they related?"

Romey shook her head at this.

"I think that he knows Mirella's brother, Atty. I believe that he is also in the house."

Pinder nodded. "That is what Reggie is telling us, when he went behind the house earlier and you were at the front door."

Another nod from Romey.

The sergeant made brief eye contact with me and gave a slight nod.

"Thank you," he said and turned to rejoin the others. He did not instruct us to get back in the van, but Romey turned to do that. I touched her elbow, she looked back at me and I held up my right hand while shaking my head, trying to convey that we would wait right there.

Louie Ragsdale couldn't sit still. Shifting his butt in the chair, he turned one way to watch the crowd, then a few seconds later, turning another way. Becky watched this for a couple of minutes. She reached over to put a hand on his shoulder. He turned to look at her.

"What's wrong?" she said. "It's something with Michael and Romey, isn't it?" He shifted again, waited a beat, trying to decide the best way to explain. He brought the chair around and folded his arms.

"OK. Let me tell you what's going on," he said.

Louie gave a rundown of all that had happened, at least all that he knew about, and what was taking place in Marsh Harbour at that very minute. He started with the voicemail and Romey telling Hanlon, then about his conversations with Inspector Knowles. Becky listened without commenting. When she thought that he'd finished, she leaned forward and crossed both her arms and rested on the table. She gave him a slow, repetitive shaking of her head.

"There is nothing that you can do, Louie. *Nothing*," she repeated.

"I know that," he said. The annoyance seemed misdirected at his wife.

"Do you?" she responded.

They were in one of their stare downs, the kind that usually ended with Louie reluctantly acknowledging that Becky was right. He looked at his watch, then looked at the crowd scattered around at the other tables. The singer was in the middle of *I Write the Songs*, not one of Louie's favorites.

"You wanna' go back to the cottage?" he asked.

Sixty
Let's Go

Cynthia Knowles, Denny Ring and three other RBPF cops were underway, now just twenty minutes from Marsh Harbour. The roof light bar and emergency flashers were all turned on. Corporal Roos was behind the wheel and he kept the van pegged at seventy-five miles per hour.

For the first ten minutes after they'd left Cooper's Town, there had been more discussion about hostage situations and what they might expect when they got there. Everyone had spoken at some point during the exchange, even if it had been only a grunt to indicate understanding and agreement.

Now all were silent. Five well-trained, disciplined, alert law enforcement veterans, looking out at the trees and silhouettes of a passing landscape and the night sky.

Knowles held her phone with both hands in her lap. Two minutes earlier she had communicated with the officers on the scene and gave their estimated time of arrival, 9:55. It was understood that phone contact would be reestablished a few minutes before they reached Marsh Harbour and that they would keep the call connected. It was also understood that as soon as they reached the turn for Bay Street, the driver would shut down the light bar.

Joey was standing at the open back door, right arm tight to his rib cage and the gun aimed at Mirella. Atty was starting to come around. He'd moved once, now was starting to push himself up onto his knees. Joey watched.

He'd seen someone across the street, maybe a policeman. It was not Terrence Williams; wasn't large enough. From the time Joey had arrived, Terrence had not been out of his thoughts. Any confrontation with the man now, especially after he'd invaded the man's home and threatened his wife, was just one of the fears tugging at Joey. He needed to reconsider the next move.

Go out through the back yard and run all the way to the docks where he would meet up with Jameson and leave the island, or, wait a few minutes to see if anything happened out front? There was no window at the front door. Only a partial view of the street was possible through a bedroom window and the view was obstructed by the corner of another house and some bushes.

If he waited any longer, someone might come to the front door. If it was the woman again, Joey could handle that. Maybe the man across the street was with her.

Atty had made it to his knees, head down and both hands feeling the back of his skull. Joey looked at Mirella, then stepped out onto the deck closer to Atty.

Mirella watched Joey go out the door to where Atty was. She wondered if her brother was still unconscious. She also knew that if she got up from the sofa that there was a greater chance that Joey would become more violent. She believed that he would shoot one or both of them.

Oh, Lord, how she prayed that Terrence was here.

Sixty One
No Shots

The plan was straight forward; do not provoke. Surround the house, contain the perimeter to ensure that the subject with the firearm does not leave. Quietly alert neighbors, no one is to come out of their home, everyone told to stay clear of windows facing the street.

Sergeant Pinder instructed the others, informed Reggie, Romey and me. He asked us to stay back and away from the street in front, but he did not tell us to get into the van. One patrol car closer to us was now pulled at an angle across the street, the other car had moved about two-hundred feet farther and would block the street a short distance beyond Mirella's house.

Pinder also told us that other RBPF officers were on the way, coming down from Cooper's Town. They were expected to arrive shortly. As soon as he said this, I looked at Romey. She knew and I knew. I motioned for to her to join me behind the van. Reggie stayed next to Pinder.

"Cross your fingers that nothing happens before they get here," I said. "As long as nobody gets jumpy," I looked back at Mirella's house, "and assuming that this Joey guy doesn't flip out, they could get it under control and have Mirella out of there unharmed."

"What about the gun? Reggie told us the man was holding a gun on Mirella," she said.

"Yes. If he knows that the police are here, or as soon as he figures it out, his best chance will be to negotiate. Unless he's crazy."

"Will they try to shoot him first?" I shook my head.

"You heard what Sergeant Pinder said. 'Do not provoke," I said, watching the house and the patrol car up the street. I turned to Romey and added, "Even if he shoots first, they're not gonna return fire. Not yet."

Romey's wasn't convinced. "How do you know that?" Anxiety was creeping back into her voice.

"One of these guys," I pointed at Pinder, "or one of the officers coming down from Cooper's Town, will try to start a dialogue. They will ask some questions and *listen* to what Joey says, try to establish rapport. As long as he has hostages, they're not going to start *demanding* that he come out with his hands up. That tactic could turn bad real fast."

Romey surprised me again. Stepping closer, with both of her hands she took hold of my arm and leaned her head on my chest. I put my right arm around her shoulder. Her hair smelled like the flowers at the beach. Mighta' been my imagination. I kissed the top of her head. Then imagined Louie's voice, 'How ya doin' down there, Hanlon?'

After a few seconds, I pulled back. She dropped her hands from my arm, took my left hand in hers and looked back at the policemen.

"I'm going to call Louie," I said. "Let him know what's happening."

Jameson heard the paddle in the water, then saw Clancy in the raft. He looked at his watch. It had now been thirty minutes since Joey had told him twenty minutes. He pulled out his phone and dialed Joey's number.

"Yah, mon. We have a problem," Joey said by way of answering. Jameson held the phone away from his ear, looked at it, then held the phone up again and responded.

"What be a problem?"

Joey was standing at the door holding the gun on Mirella and keeping an eye on Atty, who'd managed to get up and get seated in one of the plastic chairs. He kept his head down and was not talking.

"I am still here," Joey said. Jameson was only half-listening as he looked to see where Clancy was. He had beached the raft and was now standing in the shallow surf looking his way.

Jameson's plan had been for Joey to arrive well before Clancy got there. But they had also allowed time to wait on shore before going to meet the boat that would take them to Nassau. That had been Clancy's idea, watch the water, make certain that no Royal Bahamas Police Force patrol

268

boats were out.

"Starting right now," Jameson said. He looked at his watch.

"Thirty minutes. You be taking care of *your* problem." He let that sink in, then concluded with, "I still be where I told you. Then I am gone."

Slipping the phone into his front pants pocket, Jameson stepped out onto the sand and walked up the beach to meet Clancy.

The call ended. Joey slipped the phone back into his jacket along with the two other phones. He stepped onto the deck and stood over Atty.

Sixty Two
No Lights

Ragsdale answered on the first ring. He stood up and pointed at the door to show Becky that he was going out to the patio.

"What's the story?" Louie said.

"There are two patrol cars here, four cops. More on the way. I think the group that's been up at Cooper's Town is coming," Hanlon said.

"Yeah, I told her when you called earlier. They were outa' there pretty quick."

"The guy in charge here is a sergeant," Hanlon said, then added, "Older guy, looks like he knows what he's doing. Seems pretty steady." Louie had known a bunch of sergeants in his time. Many were more 'steady' than some of the higher ranking officers he'd encountered.

"These guys up here, with Knowles, none of 'em are over *forty*. Whatd'ya know about the training they're doing?" Louie said.

"Nothing, really. Why?"

"Was it tactical, incident encounter drills? Or is it all

classroom, brain-melting stuff?"

Hanlon made a groan. "Louie, I didn't interview them. *You're* the one who had the chit chat," he said. Ragsdale didn't reply.

"Why does that matter?" Hanlon asked.

"Hard to say. I talked to her twice. But I was scoping out the squad while I was at their table. Both times, I had a sense these guys were wound pretty tight. Yeah, they're off duty and havin' a beer. But I don't think anybody was relaxing and having a good time."

"I can't tell ya," Hanlon said. "I only saw them when they first arrived. So what's your point?"

Ragsdale recognized once again that Hanlon was inexperienced when it came to law enforcement tactical deployment and the level of self-discipline with individual members in any group.

"The last thing you need down there is a bunch of hotshots all pumped-up, or just *one guy*, coming in loaded for bear and ready to end it fast. That could get somebody killed," Louie said, then added, "Good chance that it would be one of the hostages. Or both."

"I don't think they do that kinda' stuff here," Hanlon said. "Everything I've seen with Bahamians, so far, and things Bill has told me, I think they're more measured. Thoughtful without being hasty. Sort of 'go with the flow.' Maybe not as likely to force a confrontation."

Ragsdale was staring at the sky out across the Sea of Abaco, listening to Hanlon babble how everything would be all right. He moved from the edge of the patio, stepped out to the lawn to get a better view of the stars. He was looking south, in the direction of where he presumed Marsh Harbour to be.

"Not much skyglow here," Ragsdale said. "I'm not seeing any lights reflected." He turned slowly, scanning the horizon. "In any direction."

"Here's the police van," Hanlon said.

"You wanna stay on the line or call me back?"

"I'll call back."

"Don't worry, mon. Be happy," Ragsdale said. He hit the end call button.

The light blue RBPF van came in quietly. I ended my call with Ragsdale. Reggie had been sitting sideways in the driver's seat of his van, door open, feet resting on the running board. He got out and stood next to Romey. They watched the police van. I stepped closer to join them.

Cynthia Knowles was first one out, followed by three guys coming from the back and the driver from the other side. All were in uniform, light blue short-sleeve shirts, dark blue pants with a wide red stripe down the outside of each leg. All of them had holstered guns

Sergeant Pinder went over to greet them. If Knowles saw us, she didn't acknowledge it. Quickly, a cluster of seven RBPF officers huddled together, plus two others farther up the street. It was all business now. Whatever their training had been all week, this was the real deal.

We could hear the back and forth conversation, mostly Pinder, then Knowles, but not the specifics of what was being discussed. After a couple of minutes, Pinder turned and looked our way. He said something to Knowles. She looked over, then started in our direction.

Romey watched her cousin and the other officers talking. Now Cyndy was coming toward her.

Over a period of almost twenty years, Romey had seen her in uniform many times. Never had she seen her look the way she did at this moment; stern, focused, not a trace of a smile. Nothing in the expression conveyed her natural warmth and humor.

"Romey, you OK?" Cyndy asked, giving her a quick hug. Romey nodded.

"I'm so glad that you came," she said. They held hands and stared into one another's eyes for a couple of seconds, then Romey added, "Mirella must be so frightened."

"Do you know about this Joey Aberle? Has Mirella talked about him before?" Cyndy said.

Romey shook her head. "She mentioned his name just once. She was worried about Atty bein' around him."

"But you don't know anything about him having trouble with police, sometime in the past?"

"Mirella jus say that he is no good," Romey said.

"She never talk about things he did," she added.

Knowles turned to Reggie and gave him a quick hug. "Nice to see you, Reggie. Thank you for being with Romey."

Reggie placed a hand on Knowles shoulder. "Been a long time, young lady," he said. Knowles then looked at Hanlon and nodded.

"You must be Michael Hanlon?" she said. He stepped over and extended his hand and they shook.

"I met your friend, Lou. At The Tipsy," she said. "He is concerned about you."

Hanlon gestured with a palms up, eyebrows arched and mouth shut response.

"And thank you for coming with Romey," Knowles said, turning away to rejoin the other policemen.

All of the officers began to retrieve gear from the back of the police van. Each of them donned a ballistic bullet-resistant vest. Two of the officers now had rifles. They moved back to assemble near the patrol car angled in the middle of the street.

Four policemen, including the two with rifles, split into pairs and moved up both sides of the street. Knowles held back, quietly talking with Sergeant Pinder. By my count, there were now six policemen near Mirella's house and one across the street a short distance from the patrol car.

A couple of minutes after the teams went up the street, Knowles removed the belt and holster holding her gun. She carefully placed them on the hood of the patrol car, removed the gun from its holster, checked the clip, then shoved the weapon into the back of her waistband below the vest. She turned and said something to Pinder.

Glancing up the street, she adjusted her hat and began walking slowly toward Mirella's house.

Sixty Three
Delay

Joey had Atty back inside and on the sofa. Looking at him from the front, he saw only a little blood on the side of Atty's neck and the top of his shirt.

While the blow may not have caused a gaping wound, it was clear that Atty was still feeling it. He'd moved awkwardly coming into the house and appeared to be stunned; his movements were slow. Joey hoped that Atty's condition would make the next step a little easier.

"You have some belts in dis house?" Joey said to Mirella. She looked at him, confused. He grabbed his own belt and wiggled it.

"Like dis," he said, pulling on his belt again. "Your husband, he is a big man. Must have some belts." Mirella nodded.

"TD, he still have clothes here? And you. You have some belts, I am sure." Another nod. Joey motioned with the gun for her to get up. She rose slowly.

"Atty. Doan you move, mon. Would not be good for her," Joey said, pointing the gun at Mirella. "Les go," he added, nudging Mirella with the gun. "Find da belts."

Atty didn't move. A couple minutes after they'd left him there on the sofa, Mirella came back to the living room with Joey behind her. He had several belts bunched together in his left hand. Joey looked around the room. He turned to the small combined kitchen/dining area. There was a table and four chairs.

"Get one of dese chairs," he said to Mirella, using the gun to direct her. She complied, pulling out a ladder back chair that had a wicker seat. Joey turned the gun like he was mixing something.

"Turn it around," he said. She turned the chair so it was facing the wall, away from the living room.

"Atty, come here," Joey said. No movement from Atty. "Now, mon," Joey shouted, waving the gun. Atty got up and moved slowly to the chair where Mirella stood.

"Sit," Joey said, tapping Mirella on the shoulder with the gun. Once again she did what she was told. Joey tapped Atty on the arm with the gun and shoved the belts toward him.

"Strap her feet to da chair," Joey said. Atty hesitated, but as soon as Joey moved the gun closer to Mirella, he took one of the belts from Joey's hand and knelt in front of Mirella.

"Put your feet together," Joey ordered. She did.

"Go on, mon," he said. Atty looped the belt around Mirella's feet, then stopped.

"Pull it back, aroun da leg on da chair. Make it tight," Joey said.

It took Atty a few seconds, but he found a way to wrap the end of the belt around one leg of the chair, brought it back through the buckle and pulled tension on it. Must've been one of Terrence's belts as it still had some length.

"Tighter," Joey said. Atty cinched it another notch and Mirella let out a whimper. Atty looked up at her.

"Das good," Joey said. "Now da hands." He dropped another belt in front of Atty, who moved slowly but didn't need more prodding.

Atty figured a way to wrap this belt, one of Mirella's, around her hands and cinch it to the back edge of the chair, forcing her arms down and around to her left side and pulling her right shoulder forward. When he'd finished, Atty straightened up and stared at Joey.

Joey had no real intention of hurting them. He only hoped to create a delay long enough to allow him to get away from the house. Get to his meeting with Jameson, get away from Abaco.

Outside someone called Mirella's name. The woman was back. Knocking at the door.

Sixty Four
Distance

Six RBPF officers were in position. Knowles very slowly approached the front of the house. She knocked on the door.

No sounds from inside, no response to the knocking. She tried again.

"Mirella. It's Cyndy Knowles. Are you home?"

Nothing.

Knowles turned her head, slowly scanning the closest neighbor's house to her left. Then she looked across the street. She knew the positions of where all of her fellow officers should be; she could see four of them. Not moving, still in front of the door, she counted to ten.

"I'm going around back, Mirella. Are you in there?"

Inspector Denny Ring was one of the officers with a rifle. Now in a prone position on the grass at the corner of a house directly opposite Mirella's front door, Ring was up on both elbows, holding the rifle at an angle in front of him. When he'd checked the sight a minute earlier, he calculated the distance at about one-hundred-fifteen-feet He could bring the rifle up and have a shot off in less than two seconds.

Knowles was speaking loud enough that he could hear what was said. She was turning now, said that she was going around back. Then she stopped and looked back at the door. She'd heard something.

Ring watched. He gave a quick glance at the officer across the street from him, near the corner of the house on Knowles' left. One other patrolmen and the other RBPF shooter were both on the back side of the house.

"Mirella is not here," Joey yelled. "Gone to find her boy."

Joey aimed the gun at Mirella but kept a close eye on Atty, now seated on the floor only three feet from his sister strapped into the chair. Eyes wide and a defiant expression on her face, Mirella didn't make sound. Joey wished that he'd had Atty put a gag on her.

At first there was no response. Joey hoped that the woman was leaving. Then she spoke again.

"Do you know when she will be back?" the woman said.

"No. She say late," Joey lied.

Silence.

We could barely see Knowles at Mirella's front door. There was no outside light on, but enough light came from the street and other houses that we could make out that she was still there. We couldn't hear what she was saying.

Romey took hold of my left hand again. Reggie stood next to us. We saw the movements of one the officers positioned next to the house abutting Mirella's property. It went unspoken, but I knew that we all shared the same fear: waiting to hear a shot.

I suspected that we also shared the hope, or a prayer, that the shot would *not* come from inside the house.

"Joey Aberle. I would like to talk with you," Knowles said. No response.

"Please. Could you come out for a minute? I am an old friend of Mirella and Terrence," she added. Nothing. She waited, again counted to ten.

"Joey. We know that you are in there. We know that Mirella and Atty are with you. Let them come out." After a couple of seconds, he responded.

"Who is with you?" the man shouted. Knowles bent her right arm at the elbow, made a fist and moved it in a sideways knocking motion, not at the door but signaling to the others that she'd engaged the man with the gun.

"I am Inspector Cynthia Knowles, Royal Bahamas Police Force. I have other officers with me." She paused, listening and waiting, then added, "We want you to let Mirella and Atty come out."

At the sound of his name, Joey froze. The reflex made him touch the trigger of the gun, but then he slowly eased the pressure back.

Atty looked up when the woman said Joey's name. Mirella's back was to him as she faced the wall. Joey stepped closer to the front door, raised the gun, aimed it at the door, then held up. He looked over his shoulder toward the back door.

"Joey, no one is going to be hurt," the woman was saying. "Let them come out. Then we will talk."

Looking at his watch, Joey pulled the phone from his jacket pocket. One of the other phones fell to the floor. He kicked at the phone and ignored it.

Jameson would not wait. He believed that. The man had explained the departure time was arranged so that they could arrive offshore from Nassau in the early morning hours.

"Joey," the woman repeated.

Knowles raised her left arm above her head and held it perfectly still, as though she was signaling for a bus to stop. It was a pre-arranged signal for Ring and the two other officers who could see her. Communication with the subject had begun. Hold your position.

With her right hand she felt for the gun on her back. She patted it, moving it up slightly in the waistband so that the grip was not impeded by her vest.

No reply from inside, but she could hear someone talking.

Sixty Five
Signal

"**Da police are here, mon,**" Joey said, voice shrill and frightened. Jameson listened. He turned to look at Clancy now sitting in the dark on the edge of the raft. Joey was prattling on about 'da police.'

"Dey know I am here. How could dis be?" Joey said.

Bèbè was the first word that came to Jameson. But Joey didn't speak Creole. In Bahamian speak, the word is *dumb*. You are dumb, Joey. That is why they know that you are there.

Joey wasn't finished talking. Jameson was no longer listening. He held the phone away from his ear and ended the call.

Making a rolling motion with his right hand to Clancy, Jameson stepped up to the raft and they began pushing it farther out in the water. They would paddle out a short distance before Clancy started the small electric motor.

No sign of the boat. It would come.

Joey moved toward the back door, then caught himself and stayed out of view. He peeked through one window, then the other. No one in sight. The woman had said 'other officers.' They would be at the back of the house, too.

It came to him. Mirella had lied. She'd said that she had called a friend earlier when Joey had caught her with the phone in the bathroom. She'd called da police.

He stood over Mirella. He had a strong urge to hit her with the gun. Atty still watched Joey but he had not tried anything.

"You call da police," Joey yelled. Mirella shook her head.

"No. I did not call them. You said that we would get hurt." Joey stared down at her. He was shaking.

"Joey," the woman outside said. "We want to talk."

Knowles had been at the door for several minutes. The officer positioned at the house next door to her left had moved in closer. From where we were standing, it looked as though he was squatting or kneeling next to the stoop a couple feet away from Knowles.

We still couldn't hear what she was saying. The only sounds came from a television or radio playing somewhere in another house and the sound of cars when they passed out on the main highway.

I did a deep cleansing breath and held it for several

seconds. Reggie turned to look at me when I exhaled, said nothing, but his eyes showed the same concern that I was feeling. Romey didn't speak, only occasionally squeezing my hand. I had a flashback.

An incident two years earlier, a living room of a condo in a small town in Connecticut. A frightened man, some cops and me. The results of that evening became part of my continuing education.

On the opposite side of the street from Mirella's house I saw movement. It was in close to one of the houses, in the front and near the ground. Had to be one of the other cops, most likely one with a rifle.

Knowles listened. No reply to her last plea. She gave it another try.

"Joey. No one needs to get hurt here. Whatever your situation is, we can talk about it." She counted to ten. "Let them come out, Joey."

"You doan know anyting about me," the man yelled.

Knowles raised her left arm and held it straight up again, another signal to the others. It was all part of the plan, the understanding being that any use of wireless communication while she was in close was not advisable.

"You are right. I don't know anything about you," she said. She *did* know that RBPF officers in Marsh Harbour knew who he was, even though he had no record of arrests.

"But this is not what we want to happen," Knowles

286

added. She kept her voice measured, not allowing it to match the tone that he was using.

"Holding people against their will. We don't want to do that, Joey." Constant use of his name and the inclusive 'we' was part of the negotiating tactics. Establish some minimum level of trust.

No response.

She would wait to remind him that they were aware of his possession of a gun. Do not provoke. Knowles counted to ten. As long as we are talking, do not rush.

The two officers at the rear of the house adjusted their positions, one man now closer to the small deck and ready to move on signal, the other shooter with a rifle now just thirty feet away and in a direct line with the back door.

Any signal to initiate action would come from Knowles. She would pull her gun, hold both arms high above her head and briefly cross her hands, then quickly drop both arms. The relay of that signal would come from the officer at the street, just beyond the house, who was visible to all other officers.

If this happened, Knowles and the officer closest to the front would move immediately to enter the door. The officer in the street would join the rush at the back door while both shooters would hold their positions should the subject make his way out.

Something happens before Knowles gave any signal

to move in, such as shots being fired by the subject through the door or a window, the whole scenario would change instantly. The police entry would then come from the opposite direction from where shots were being fired. If that happened, the dual objective was to *protect* the hostages and *eliminate* any further threat from the subject.

Knowles stayed at the front door. As long as there was no gunfire, no indication from inside the house that the hostages were being harmed, she was prepared to wait as long as it took. She inhaled and counted to ten again.

"Joey. Let me come inside."

Sixty Six
Light

All of a sudden the door was open. After no response, Knowles had waited another ten seconds. Then the door opened. A large young man stood there holding the door knob. No gun visible.

It took her a second to process that this must be Mirella's brother, Atty. They stared at one another. Critical decision time. Knowles patted twice on the front of her vest, a signal. She took a tentative step forward.

"I'm coming in, Joey," she said. Atty remained there holding the door open. Knowles took three slow, careful steps. She was inside. Across the room Mirella was seated in an awkward position, both arms pulled to one side as though she were hiding something. Knowles saw Mirella's feet were strapped to the leg of the chair.

Joey stepped out from behind a side wall, gun raised in both hands aimed at Knowles. She slowly put her hands in the air. No one said a word.

One of the officers across the street ran to the front of the house. He joined the other cop who'd been there with Knowles. The two of them stood against the wall, one on each side of the open door.

Denny Ring moved quickly down to the edge of the street, went to one knee and held the rifle across his left leg. Now just ten feet away from him, the officer in the street responsible for relaying signals to the others, stood with his gun drawn, left arm raised. Any shots or an indication of trouble, he would give the 'go' signal.

On the back deck, another officer now stood to the side of the door. He could see Knowles inside with her hands raised, saw a man standing at the front door, but could not see who was holding a gun.

We saw quick movement from two RBPF officers across the street, then there was light coming from inside the front door. I could see movement but couldn't tell who or what. My guess was that Knowles had gone inside.

Reggie looked at me. I crossed my fingers and raised my hand for him to see. He nodded, then turned back to watch the house.

"What happened?" Romey said.

"I think they've gone inside," I said.

Still nothing coming from the house.

Then, a man's voice. I couldn't hear what he said. The door closed.

"**Close da door,**" Joey yelled. Atty pushed the door closed and turned around. Joey gave a quick, short jerk with the gun.

"Go back dare," he yelled. Atty moved slowly past Knowles and lowered himself onto the sofa.

Joey moved to his right and was now directly in front of Knowles. Almost at point blank range, or close enough that he could strike her with the gun if wanted to.

"You say dat others are wit you," Joey said. "How many police?"

"Six," Knowles replied. Joey did a quick glance over his shoulder at the back door.

"Dey waiting to shoot me," he said, then gave a nervous, high pitched laugh.

"No one needs to get hurt," Knowles repeated. Joey glared at her.

After twenty minutes of terror and the last few hours of fear and anger, Mirella spoke up.

"We have not done anything to you. You said that you did not want to hurt Atty. We cannot hurt you." Joey looked at Mirella, then at Atty. He shook his head, again the nervous laugh.

"Dat change if Terrence be here," Joey said.

"Terrence is on Eluthera. I told you dat," Mirella said. "He is not comin' back until tomorrow." She prayed that he was on his way this very minute.

"Joey, let Mirella and her brother leave. I will stay right here," Knowles said.

This caused Joey to hesitate a beat. The gun lowered perhaps two inches but was clearly still at an angle that any shot would hit Knowles center body. He continued staring at her. She nodded.

"Let them go," Knowles said. Joey looked at Atty.

"Take da belts off her," he said, motioning with the gun to Mirella.

Atty rose slowly from the sofa and went to his sister. First he released the belt binding her hands, then knelt down to unstrap her feet. When he finished, Atty stood next to her chair. Mirella rubbed her wrists and moved her right shoulder back and forth.

"Open da door, Atty." Joey said. He raised the gun back to a dead aim on Knowles and added, "You tell dem not to shoot." She nodded. Atty was moving to the door.

"Go wit him," Joey shouted at Mirella. She got up from the chair and tried not to run. Knowles watched over her left shoulder. As soon as Atty put his hand on the knob, she shouted to the officers outside.

"Coming out. Hold your fire. Unarmed. Coming out, NOW," she repeated.

As she passed Knowles, Mirella whispered, "Thank you."

The door was open. Atty went out first, Mirella right behind. Each of the RBPF officers outside the door took them by the arm and pulled them away from the door.

Joey waived the gun at Knowles. "Close da door," he

yelled. She backed up slowly and raising her left leg, caught the door with her toe and pushed it closed.

"Joey, can I put my hands down?" she asked.

Sixty Seven
No Good

Someone came through the door. Then another person was coming out. There was movement at the side of the door, then the two who came out moved away quickly, we couldn't see them.

"Here we go," I said. Romey stepped forward trying to get a better look.

It was too dark and too far for us to see who came out of the house. All that we could see was some rapid movement and, for a few seconds, light from inside. As had happened earlier, the door closed.

"Did you see who came out?" I asked Reggie. He shook his head, but held up two fingers.

"Not sure. Looks like a man, den a woman. Maybe Mirella," he said. Romey took my arm again.

"But it was two?" I asked, wondering if Knowles was still inside. Reggie nodded.

"Dat's what I saw." He again held up the fingers.

As Reggie said this, coming down the street toward us was a woman, moving quickly. She was about Romey's size. Then right behind her was a larger man. Behind them came an RBPF officer, one of the first to arrive on the scene. He had his gun drawn, right arm across his chest.

When they were about ten feet away, Romey started to go to the woman. I reached out and took her arm holding her back.

"Better wait," I said. She did, for all of two seconds, then ran to the woman and hugged her.

Knowles felt relief that the hostages were out of the house. She knew that her next move would make all the difference in her proclamation 'no one needs to get hurt.'

Joey had allowed her to lower her hands. When Mirella and Atty were gone and Knowles had pushed the door closed, Joey had taken a couple of steps backward in the direction of the back door. Now they were a few feet apart. Knowles kept her hands visible at her side.

"Joey," she began slowly, "what is this all about?" When she asked the question she flexed her hands hoping that the gesture would help to get Joey to start talking. He shook his head.

"Dis all no good," he said. For the first time since she entered the house, he was not threatening her with the gun. Joey started pacing, head down and moving back and forth slowly.

Do not provoke. Knowles wouldn't make a sudden move to spook him. Empathy. Listen, maintain rapport.

He shook his head. She waited, then spoke slowly.

"What is no good?" she said. No response.

"Why were you holding Mirella and her brother?"

Joey's eyes flashed at Knowles and he stopped pacing. He studied her for a second.

"You know bout dem boys who be shot?" he said. She waited before responding.

"What boys?" she said, voice soft, no emotion.

"Dey want me to steal da boat for *dem*. Den dey want to cheat me," he said. His eyes pleaded for understanding. They stood looking at one another.

It clicked. Knowles knew about the two Haitians who'd been shot. She knew that one of them had since died. Now she knew that Joey was somehow involved, maybe the one who shot them. And now she knew 'what this was all about.' Another pause, then she spoke again in the same, level tone.

"Joey, we can work on this," she said. Craning his neck backward, looking up at the ceiling, he began shaking his head again.

"Dis is too late," he said. Now he was holding both hands to his head, shaking, the gun next to his right ear. He began to sob.

"Joey, drop the gun," Knowles said. He stopped and looked at her. She was in a shooter's stance, gun gripped in her right hand and supported with her left, dead aim on Joey. He didn't move.

"Joey, put the gun down," she repeated. "I do not want to shoot you."

The man who came out of the house with Mirella, I learned that it *was* her brother, was now leaning against the back fender of the RBPF van, head down, not talking to anyone. Romey and Mirella were standing close together, not far from him. Romey was holding both of Mirella's hands and they were whispering. The officer who'd brought the two out had gone back to the house. Reggie and I were still watching.

The front door opened again, we could see the light inside. Then there was movement outside, from policemen on both sides of the street. Someone came out of the house, someone tall. Then another person came out.

Within a few minutes, coming down the street toward us were two policemen. They had a tall man walking between them, his hands appeared to be cuffed behind his back. Then Knowles was coming down the street. Next to her was a policemen carrying a rifle. They were followed by two more RBPF officers, one of them also carrying a rifle.

As soon as the first local patrol car left, transporting Joey Aberle, Inspector Knowles and the four others who had made the trip from Cooper's Town loaded into their van and headed for the Marsh Harbour station. Two of the local cops hung back to speak with Mirella and Atty.

Initially Joey would be held in Marsh Harbour and charged with unlawful restraint, possession of an illegal firearm and threatening by the use of a firearm. For the next hour or so, Knowles would continue the dialogue with Joey in hopes of obtaining more information about the shooting of the two Haitians. She had not yet told him that one of the men was dead.

The police report on holding against their will and the eventual release of Mirella Williams and Atty Gilbert, as well as the ultimate surrender without incident by Aberle, would come later.

The RBPF officers involved had performed skillfully, efficiently and professionally. Outside the force, that might not get a lot of attention. Although the events had *not* been part of the small group training sessions of the past week, a successful resolution of the incident in Marsh Harbour would certainly gain the attention of the Commissioner and other top brass in Nassau.

Romey decided that she would stay with Mirella and Atty. Reggie volunteered to come back and bring her to Treasure Cay in the morning.

When we hugged, Romey held the embrace longer than I would have expected. For a second, I thought that she might cry. She didn't.

"It's gonna' be OK," I said, then added, "Really." She looked up and smiled. I shook my head.

"Don't say it."

She gave me a soft kiss and we hugged again. I watched her go back to the house with Mirella, Atty and the two RBPF officers.

On the ride back with Reggie, we didn't talk a lot about what we'd just witnessed. I fell into my interviewer's mindset and asked him questions about his life, his work, his family and Abaco. He seemed happy to respond to everything that I could think to ask him. By the time he dropped me at the cottage, I thought that this guy could be a goodwill tourist rep for Treasure Cay and all of Abaco.

We agreed that I would go with him in the morning to get Romey. Reggie looked at me for a second.

"You have a driver's license?" he said.

"Yes."

"Don't Romey have a car at da resort?"

"Yeah, I'm pretty sure that her car is there." He held his hands up, pointed at me and made the motion of steering a car.

"Sure," I said. "I could drive her car back to Marsh Harbour." One minor problem. "But the keys are with *her*."

"No worry. I bet she have da hide-a-key," he said.

"OK. I'll give her a call in the morning. Then I will call you, yes?"

"Dat can work. You have my card," he said, starting to retrieve another one from his visor.

"I have it, inside."

"OK, you have a good night, Michael Hanlon." He slipped the van into gear.

"Thank you, Reggie."

Approaching the door to the cottage, I thought how

Ragsdale was going to react when I told him about all of this. I'd called him when it was over and the cops were still sorting things out. He'd said that he would wait up.

I made a bet with myself that when I told him about Reggie, Louie would come up with some clever observation or a variation for Reggie's business card, something along the lines of 'Ambassador With a Gun.'

Sixty Eight
No Surprise

Two bartenders at The Tipsy were winding it down. The waitresses and busboys had most of the tables cleared, the music coming from the speakers was pre-recorded. The singer and the keyboard player were long gone.

Nearly all of the crowd had called it a night. Only two older couples remained at a table. One of the men in that foursome was still quite animated, but the other three were showing signs of packing it in. Another Thursday, another heavy run on dough, sauce, cheese and an extensive variety of toppings. And another stellar performance by the staff. Only four more of these were scheduled for the remainder of the year. January would launch a new weekly slice of Abaco's Largest Social Event.

The only reason to run newspaper ads was for first-time tourists. All of the locals, all of the returning boaters, and certainly all of the returning vacationers anticipated this outing in a way similar to how others might plan for the weekly gathering of a social club or civic group.

Pizza Night. Tee shirts available soon.

Becky Ragsdale was asleep. Louie was almost asleep, slouched on the sofa watching a Bahamian religious show on TV, volume on mute. Then he heard Hanlon at the door. Barefoot and slow, he went to let him in.

Hanlon only bugged his eyes and mumbled "Hey" as he came inside. He went straight to a chair and dropped. Louie went back to where he'd been stretched out on the wicker sofa.

"All tidied up, huh?" Louie said.

"Guess you could say that."

"What's the story on the guy with the gun? Some family dispute?" I shook my head.

"I don't think so. Best I could make out from one of the local cops, the guy had a connection to the brother. Just happened that Romey's friend, Mirella, got caught in the middle," I said.

"You said no shots fired?" he asked. I took a deep breath.

"Correct. Apparently Inspector Knowles was the one who got him to surrender."

"Huh," Louie responded. He stared at the TV, then added, "Doesn't surprise me. She looks like a pretty cool number. Those guys keep her around they might learn some things."

"Yep, sounds right," I said.

"So what'll they charge the guy with? I'm bettin' the gun was dirty," he said.

"Reggie has it as 'unlawful restraint, holding persons against their will, making threats with a firearm," I said. "Don't know about the gun."

Louie looked at the TV again. For the first time I looked at what he was watching on the screen without any sound. I watched it for a minute.

"What's this?" I said.

He chuckled. "I'm gonna' send 'em money. They're really into it."

He hit the power button, the screen went blank and Louie stood up. He stretched his arms high above his head and gave a wide, silent yawn.

"You can tell me the rest in the morning," he said. "Becky will want to hear it."

"Wait'll I fill you in on Reggie. Lot more there than meets the eye."

"Great. Can't wait to hear it." He went off to bed.

A familiar sensation came over me. My mind needed to review it all, see if I'd missed anything.

I went to the refrigerator and poured a glass of orange juice, then went out to the patio. Great sky, stars everywhere.

Plopping into one of the patio chairs, I put my feet up and for a long time replayed the entire evening, from standing with Romey outside The Tipsy before we'd gone to Marsh Harbour, through every move by the police, and concluding with my conversation with Reggie on the drive back.

There was not one thing that I'd observed by the RPBF officers that failed to impress me. Earlier, when Louie had expressed a concern that someone might over-react and push the situation in the wrong direction, my response to him had been based merely on a hunch. From what I had observed, generally speaking and only over a period of a few days, I couldn't *imagine* Bahamians acting in haste, especially in a volatile situation. Then maybe one should not generalize, eh?

Standing and watching the sky for a few minutes, I did a slow, wide scan of all of the stars that were visible. I thought about Romey.

It was late. I went inside and got ready for bed.

Sixty Nine
Tears/Sleep

Reggie was right, Romey did have a hide-a-key on her car. It was a plastic case with a magnet hidden on the back of her license plate and not easy to get at. When I managed to remove it I could see that it would be unlikely that it might accidentally dislodge and the case fall off.

After we'd finished coffee and cinnamon buns at Café LaFlorence, I left Louie and Becky to enjoy the rest of their morning while I took Romey's car to Marsh Harbor. Adjusting to steering on the right was not all that difficult. I took it easy, the drive was forty-two minutes, getting me to Marsh Harbour at five minutes after ten.

The GPS on my phone directed me to the turn-off. I sort of recognized the houses from the previous night. Pulling in behind the car that Romey had told us belonged to Mirella, I was just getting out when Romey appeared at the front door. She gave a little wave, like maybe I would forget which house it was? No.

Mirella looked the way you would expect someone to look who'd had the experience she had had over the past twenty-four hours. Shoulders slumped, arms drooping, puffy eyes and moving at the speed of a turtle. She was really beat, but tried to put on a good front. The house was quiet and I saw no sign of the younger brother.

The three of us stood in her kitchen for a few minutes talking, mostly about this being my first visit to Abaco. I volunteered that the bone fishing in The Marls had been a lot of fun, but that the visit to the blue hole and a beach picnic were the highlights, so far. This produced a smile from Romey.

"Next time, my Terrence can take you fishing," Mirella said.

"That'd be great," I said. "I've heard that he is one of the best guides around." Mirella made a little chuckling sound and looked at Romey.

"Terrence is *the best* on Abaco. Jus ask him."

"OK."

"We should go," Romey said. She and Mirella hugged, then Mirella shook my hand.

"It was nice to meet you Michael," she said, holding my hand for a minute.

"I am sorry for what you went through. I'm glad that it turned out OK," I said.

"We shall see," she replied.

Romey asked if I would drive. She was clearly exhausted, as well. The discussion on the drive to Treasure Cay was at about half the pace of normal conversations. She talked like a person just coming around from anesthesia, slow and deliberate, with delayed pauses when she was responding.

I learned that the two of them had been awake talking most of the night. Romey had dozed briefly while sitting on the sofa earlier this morning. Mirella's son, TD Junior, had come home after Mirella had called him very early in the morning. Romey's take was that he had been completely stunned.

"Total disbelief," Romey said. "His mouth open, like he was in a trance. But he hugged his mama. I think he was crying a little bit, too."

Just before I had arrived, she said, TD had taken Atty to the Marsh Harbour police station where he would be asked a lot more about his friendship with Joey Aberle. She told me that Mirella had spent a long time on the phone very early this morning when Terrence had called. Apparently he'd heard a voicemail from last night from Mirella and was 'going crazy.'

"Mirella was crying a lot. They talked and talked. That is when I dozed off," she said. She laughed and added, "Lots of 'I love you, baby' before Mirella put the phone down."

I looked over at Romey. She had her head back, eyes half-open.

"Well what would *you* say?" I asked. "Of course she's gonna say 'I love you baby'.

Romey reached over and patted my hand on the steering wheel.

"Dey been together a long time," she said.

We didn't talk during the last ten minutes before coming to the roundabout near the cottages. Romey was asleep. As soon as the car came to a stop in the parking lot, she opened her eyes and looked around.

"Are you going to be OK to drive home?" I said. She nodded.

"Um-hmm." She unfastened her seat belt and opened the passenger door.

We stood next to the car for a minute and didn't say much before Romey was about to get back in to make her five-minute drive home. She placed her hands on my shoulders and gazed at me.

"Thank you," she said, and put her head on my chest.

We embraced for maybe a full minute, still not talking. Then I pulled back and looked at her.

"You are a good friend for Mirella. I am really glad for what you did last night and that no one was hurt."

"*Real-ly*," she offered, then she gave me one of her lovely, soft kisses. I tried not to moan.

Seventy
Next

Well before first light on a cool Friday morning off New Providence island, the RBPF marine patrol intercepted a 25-foot Parker carrying two men, both believed to be Haitian nationals. The boat had been cruising at a very slow speed and running without lights.

Two officers boarded the vessel and after questioning both the man driving the boat and his passenger, decided that further questioning would be in order. One of the RBPF officers took control of the boat and brought it into the marina in Nassau. The unexpected late night call from the police station in Marsh Harbour had provided a good tip.

The passenger's name was Jameson Debois, according to a passport issued from Port au Prince, Haiti. The man operating the boat said that his name was Pierre Stephanne. He had no papers. They would be detained at RBPF headquarters on East Street subject to further investigation.

Joey Aberle quickly confessed to having stolen a boat, shooting two men that he said had promised to pay him for the boat, and finally to the charges lodged against him for the incident in Marsh Harbour at a private home. This included possession of an illegal firearm, ranked high on the priority list of offenses one might commit in the Bahamas.

Joey was just as quick to tell police that Atty Gilbert had played no role in either stealing the boat or shooting the men, that he merely had been tagging along with his friend. The police would make a determination through their ongoing investigation.

The fact that one of the men shot by Joey had died a few days after being taken into custody was going to make his case a lot more serious than perhaps he realized, self-defense aside. He would have to have an attorney, but was facing the very real prospect of a lengthy jail sentence.

Inspector Cynthia Knowles and her fellow RBPF officers, despite a late night and some extra-curricular activities, were fresh and sharp on Friday morning. They were scheduled for a brief 'going home' critique before leaving Cooper's Town.

All ten officers were better for the four-day training session. The force would be improved by their expanded perceptions, new skills and the experience gained here. Even if the gathering managed to stay off the media radar and the public got only sketchy details at some later date, Commissioner Ellison Greenslade knew that this group was the future of the Royal Bahamas Police Force.

Seated on a bench in the sun outside the Treasure Cay International Airport terminal, Louie Ragsdale, somewhat timidly, acknowledged to his wife, "Yeah, I'd come back."

"Just for the fishing?" Becky asked.

"Nah. That's a pretty nice beach."

Barring airport delays once back in the states, they could be home in Vermont, pick up the dogs and be back in their own bed before midnight.

Reggie Sayle has decided to retire from his security gig and devote full time to his family, calling on his laid-back approach to unforeseeable events and everyday life in general. There will be thousands of visitors coming to Abaco in the months and years ahead. Many of them will have an opportunity to meet Reggie and receive the 'ambassadorial' treatment, sure to score big points on their vacation tally.

Michael Hanlon will remain on Abaco until the end of November. Romey McIntosh will be back at work this very afternoon. The long range forecast calls for sunny days, temperatures expected to be in the low 80s through Thanksgiving.

Next week, another Pizza Night. Hanlon expects to go with moderation on the Goombay Smash, but also plans to experiment. Bananas are a great source of potassium.

And there is at least one more inland blue hole on the south end of the island.

AUTHOR'S NOTE: The Right Honourable Hubert Ingram, former Prime Minister, and the Royal Bahamas Police Force Commissioner, Ellison Edroy Greenslade, are the real deal.

However, they did **_not_** really make the appearances portrayed in this story. Thoughts, observations, comments or quotes attributed to them were created by me.

<u>Acknowledgements</u>:

- *Money Machine* – Gucci Mane, featuring Rick Ross
  (10/16 – Atlantic Records)
- *Old School Bahamian* – Sweet Emily and Ronnie Butler
  (11/11 – DJ Sampler, Nassau)
- *Bonefish Folley* - Phil Stubbs song (based on the legendary
  Bahamas fishing guide, Israel "Bonefish Folley" Rolle)
- *Love Train* – The O'Jays (1/73 – Philadelphia)
- *Chuck E.'s in Love* – Rickie Lee Jones (4/79 – Warner)
- *New York, New York* – Liza Minnelli (6/77 – Capitol) and
  Frank Sinatra (5/80 - Reprise)
- *You're Sixteen* – Johnny Burnette (10/60 – Liberty) and
  Ringo Starr (12/73 – Apple)
- *You'll Never Find Another Love Like Mine* – Lou Rawls
  (6/76 – Liberty)
- *My Cherie Amour* – Stevie Wonder (5/69 – Tamla)
- *Louie, Louie* – Richard Berry & The Pharaohs (6/57 – Flip)
  and The Kingsmen (11/63 – Wand)
- *I Write The Songs* – Barry Manilow (11/75 – Arista)

Thank you for the music.

- Kalick (Commonwealth Brewery, Nassau)
- BarometerBob.org (really helpful website)
- *National Geographic* (www.nationalgeographic.com) see
  August, 2010, Andrew Todhunter and Wes C. Skiles
- *Gonzo Papers Vol. 1 - The Great Shark Hunt*
  Hunter S. Thompson (Summit Books)
- *Gee's Bend - The Women And Their Quilts*
  John Beardsley, William Arnett, Paul Arnett, Jane Livingston
  (Tinwood Books - check your library)
- *Northern Exposure* – Joshua Brand and John Falsey
  (1990-95, lots of awards – CBS)
- Glamma (blog post submitted under the name Cheyennede)
- *Abaco Life* (www.abacolife.com)
- the abaconian (www.theabaconian.com)
- THE NASSAU Guardian (www.thenassauguardian.com)

ABOUT THE AUTHOR

The author is an award winning former broadcaster living in Vermont. He began his radio career as a news reporter covering both municipal and state government meetings, political campaigns, everyday community events and the incidents which frequently made the lead story of the day.

Many characters, conversations and real life experiences have inspired much of what you read in these books, but *the stories are fiction*.

www.nemysteries.com

Next up in the New England Mystery series:

- *A Hot Afternoon in MASSACHUSETTS*
(Spring 2017)

Read excerpts on the following page.

Excerpts from

A Hot Afternoon in MASSACHUSETTS

By the time they would clear the beach I knew that my evening plans were about to change.

Walking back to the car to check on Rocco, I told the cop where I was going and that I would return.

The Sandwich Police Chief had arrived. His guys on the scene had been there for nearly an hour. It was obvious that I would have to go through the story again. Maybe I should start carrying my little digital recorder with me all the time.

Wait, Hanlon. Breakthrough! People actually use their smartphones to record everything these days.

"Look it up, hotshot. Nobody ever has – and nobody ever *will* – do a better version of that song. Period," Louie said.

Ragsdale was never shy about his opinions when it came to pop music. Never mind the inconvenient fact that his tastes in music, kind of like mine, were slogging around in another era.

"You know, I once heard this local band at a club in Morgantown, West Virginia. They were pretty good," I said.

"Oh, I'll just bet they were. Made the cover of *Rolling Stone*, right?"

CONTACT:

threeriversgroupvt@gmail.com